John Saunders

Israel Mort, Overman

Vol. II: A Story of the Mine

John Saunders

Israel Mort, Overman
Vol. II: A Story of the Mine

ISBN/EAN: 9783744739115

Printed in Europe, USA, Canada, Australia, Japan

Cover: Foto ©Andreas Hilbeck / pixelio.de

More available books at **www.hansebooks.com**

ISRAEL MORT, OVERMAN

A STORY OF THE MINE

BY

JOHN SAUNDERS

AUTHOR OF 'ABEL DRAKE'S WIFE' 'HIRELL.' ETC.

IN THREE VOLUMES

VOL. II.

HENRY S. KING & CO., LONDON

1876

CONTENTS

OF

THE SECOND VOLUME.

———•◦•———

ISRAEL MORT.

CHAPTER I.

EXACT to his word Israel presented himself next day at the Farm to demand his commission money.

But he had scarcely entered within the exterior gate when he heard Griffith Williams call out loudly from the terrace above,

'There are thieves here! Shsh, Keeper! At 'em!'

Israel glanced round, looking for a place of safety, or for means of defence.

Close by his feet was a piece of ornamental rock work. Could he detach from it a manageable weapon?

VOL. II. B

In his younger days one of his favourite sports
had been that of betting on his superior strength
of hand and arm. He would often challenge men
seemingly more powerful than himself to a contest, where he undertook to lift on one hand
above his head as much as his competitors could
lift with both hands to the same position.

Grasping now the likeliest-looking piece, he
drew it forth by sheer strength from the mortar
in which it was so firmly bedded, and waited with
it ready.

In an instant Israel found himself face to face
with the Squire's favourite dog; a mastiff of rare
beauty and strength: and still more remarkable
for the contrast between his gentleness when at
rest, and his ferocity when roused by his master's
voice to attack.

Israel stood still, leaning backwards, seemingly
as impassive as the death that might here lie in
wait for him. His concentrated attitude; with
the left arm against the breast, the bent fingers
ready for the clutch; the right with the piece of
rock poised at the level of his shoulder; expectant;
might have been a study for a sculptor, of vigo-

rous, wily, feline strength; and of stern, calculated courage, and purpose.

The dog sprang, but at almost the same moment the armed hand shot out with resistless force and unerring aim at the creature's head, striking a terrific blow; meant, however, more to guard their owner, and to stop, perhaps stun, the mastiff, than with any expectation of disabling him.

Israel then sprang aside, as conscious of—and to evade—the unspent impetus of the attack. But the dog slipped, fell—how he had no leisure to consider. All he could think of, and all that Griffith Williams, standing on the terrace above, saw, was the dog pinned to the ground, his throat in the iron grasp of a hand, which evidently was squeezing all breath and life out of him, while the other hand battered the creature's head with the rock.

'Rascal!' shouted Griffith Williams. 'Let the dog go. Do you hear?'

But seeing that Israel paid no sort of attention to him, and that he was killing the animal he so much valued, inch by inch, minute by minute, by sheer force of strangulation, (using now both hands

for that purpose,) and in an almost awful silence,
he called to his other dogs, forgetting they were
shut up—called for his servants, and, getting no
immediate reply, ran for his gun.

By the time he had got it, and felt it, and
realised the danger of the temptation he was
running into, he had taken second thoughts, so he
put it back: and then ran along the terrace and
down the short flight of steps to confront Israel,
and see if he could yet save his dog.

He found the pair still in the same position,
except that Israel had sunk on to one knee during
the terrible struggle, the better to retain that
unrelaxing. remorseless grasp on which his very
life, he felt. depended.

Never for a moment had he allowed eye, or
thought, or will, to diverge from that brute
antagonist. But now, aware of footsteps behind,
he turned his head half round. saw the dog's
owner, looked again at the dog. who was panting,
exhausted, all but motionless at last; then he rose
again slowly to his feet, still retaining his hold and
his bent posture, then he let go, and jumped
suddenly and swiftly upon the dog with the whole
weight of his body, whose entrails burst forth.

And then he turned, 'cool as a cucumber,' to use his own phrase in speaking of David's cheeks, in the first chapter of this narrative, and said breathlessly,

'A fine dog, that, Mr. Griffith Williams! I am glad it wasn't mine, for I should miss him.'

Griffith Williams looked from the shocking picture of his dog—who was not dead, but moaned helplessly as if asking to be allowed to die—to Israel's face; then said, almost below his breath, unconscious awe and respect modifying his intense hate,

'Are you man or devil?'

'That's as people use me.'

'What do you want here?'

'Want? I thought gentlemen generally paid respect to appointments.'

'I made no appointment.'

'No; but I take people as I find 'em, and knowing your ways I made one for you yesterday, as you know very well.'

'What do you want?' savagely demanded Griffith Williams.

'Seven hundred and fifty pounds for commission on the sale of the mine.'

' And if I refuse ? '

' You can't.'

' Can't, eh ! ' And therewith the Squire broke out into a prolonged and very loud laugh.

' You can't,' reiterated Israel.

' Why ? '

' I should have thought, sir, your own interest and comfort would have told you why. But since they don't, perhaps you will be good enough to listen to my notions. You are an educated gentleman ; I am only an ignorant collier. Excuse me, then, if I put things a bit roughly while making them plain.'

' If you reflect without anger or prejudice on all that has passed, you will see—you can't help it— that at the beginning I advised you for the best ; that I acted in a prompt, straight forrud manner, and that I needed only to be met in the same way, for all to have gone right between us. But what happened ? First you were eager, hot upon the whole business, then all of a sudden you grow cool ; you see lions in every bush where I never yet seed anything bigger than a hare ——.'

' Hark ye, Israel. Be content to have robbed

me. Don't add insult lest ——.' Griffith Williams' face showed with what difficulty he had refrained thus far from using violence.

'You see, Mr. Williams, I haven't such a vocabu· lary of choice words to choose from as you have, nor such skill in selecting only the amiablest thoughts wherewith to do one's business. I aint a student of human natur'.'

'D—n you! How much longer do you mean to annoy me? Will you go?'

'Presently. Where was I? Oh, I reck'lect! Well, sir, when I found I couldn't move you on nohow, nor see no certain end of any kind, I did begin to speckilate on my own account; and when once I begin things I generally goes on with them, as I did with you, by the shortest road to the most sartin end. What's the consequence? Why, that whereas I should have had with you some hundreds a year, and no more—though all the same I'd been a faithful and contented servant —'

'That's a lie,' roared Griffith.

'No; it's true—*for a time.* I'd been contented for a reasonable time, but now being obligated to take another path—one I didn't want at first to go into—what's the result? Why I have all you meant to give me, and I'm owner of a third of the mine into the bargain.'

'Owner! A third of the mine!' almost gasped Griffith.

'My own arnin'! My own honest arnin'! You agreed to sell for fifteen thousand pounds; Mrs. Jehoshaphat agreed to give twenty-two thousand five hundred pounds, which, as you will see on reckoning, left me seven thousand five hundred pounds, or a third.'

'And you have the hardihood to come here and tell me this to my face?'

'Why not?'

'Why not? My God, what a scoundrel! Israel, you may perhaps take it as a compliment, but I really don't know whether your impudence or your infamy most strikes me.'

'"Infamy" and "scoundrel" are actionable words, Mr. Griffith.'

'I am delighted to hear it, and you may rely upon it, *Mr.* Mort, that I shall give you the opportunity of obtaining any number of witnesses.

For that which I call you now, I will proclaim you to the world—a truly infamous scoundrel.'

'Well,' remarked Israel, after a pause, 'I suppose we must agree to differ about what you will do in that, as we differ as to what you will do in this matter of the commission.'

'Yes; and when I pay you that, you may expect me to be silent about the other. Good morning, Mr. Mort.'

'Good morning, Mr. Griffith Williams. I am sorry you should put yourself to fresh expenses, but, of course, if you do, you'll own as a gentleman I wasn't to blame, because I warned you.'

CHAPTER II.

ILLUSTRATING AN OLD PROBLEM.

NEXT day Griffith received a lawyer's letter repeating Israel's demand; and signed—Keppel North.

The day after, this was answered by Griffith's solicitor, Mr. Spettigue, requesting, in most polite terms, a meeting.

The two men of law met. The agreement was shown. It was confessed by Griffith's own adviser that he had not a leg to stand on, and that there could only be a general laugh at his expense if the matter became public.

'The neatest thing I ever saw done in the course of a longish life,' said that gentleman, with subdued enjoyment. 'But he's deaf to all reason.'

'Do you mean he refuses to complete the sale?' asked Mr. North.

'No ; he yields to that. He sees resistance to be hopeless.'

'But refuses the commission?'

'He does, absolutely.'

'Then my orders are not to lose an hour, or a chance, but to proceed regardless of cost.'

'You mean that, Mr. North?'

'Israel Mort means it! If you knew the man, I should need say no more. Well, I am sorry for all I see that will grow out of this business, but if war is meant it's no use calling it peace. So good morning.'

'Stay! Can't we compromise? I am willing to take some risk.'

'You mean act first, and consult your client afterwards.'

'Yes.'

'Well, suppose I tell you that I did put the idea of meeting you half way to Israel only an hour ago.'

'And he said — ' queried Mr. Spettigue.

'If I took a single sixpence less than the whole demand, he should look to me for the payment of that sixpence.'

'Dear me! dear me! My client won't move, and yours will make him. It reminds one of the pretty antique problem—What will happen when irresistible force comes into contact with immoveable strength?'

Both laughed, and beneath the laugh both saw what must be the end; which, however, it was not easy for one of the gentlemen to accept.

'I shall lose my client, even if I get back my money,' said Mr. Spettigue.

'I think not,' said the other, 'for your client is one of those men, I judge, who *will* make mistakes, and must pay for them, but doing so would like still to have somebody else to blame. Your shoulders are broad, and can bear.' The other laughed as he rejoined,

'My own thoughts run so much in that same direction, that I think I shall settle it. I almost think I shall.'

The other said nothing, for he felt silence was best. And so after a little fussing about, seeking papers, calling in a clerk to attend to things that demanded immediate attention, stirring the fire, and making remarks about the weather—all of which were perfectly understood to be but so many opportunities for turning the whole subject over a second time before making an irrevocable decision—Mr. Spettigue sat down to his writing-table, drew forth his cheque book, and presently gave Israel's adviser the whole sum demanded.

'Come now,' said the latter, when he had pocketed the valuable document, 'you don't mean to say you really have no authority for doing this?'

'Well, one doesn't care to be thought a fool in the profession, even though that might balance and modify the being so often thought a rogue out of it, so I will tell you. When I had argued the matter out with him, and had come away to act upon his policy, he came after me, and said, "Mind, if you do yield to such an infamous demand, I don't say I won't repay you, but I shall always declare that I never consented to it."'

The lawyers looked at each other significantly, laughed and separated.

CHAPTER III.

ACTION FOR LIBEL.

JUST one month and a day later, the same lawyers met again on business connected with the same clients.

Griffith Williams had been as good, or as bad, as his word, in spite of the discreet warnings of his adviser, and the pleadings of his wife, who was willing to forgive and forget anything for peace. He had told everybody he met how he had been swindled by Israel's false facts, dishonest opinions, and treacherous behaviour.

Israel heard of these things during the first week, and grimly smiled to himself.

'If those laugh who win,' thought he, 'those who lose may very well be angry. People will understand all that. His railing won't hurt me.'

And at first Israel was right. The neighbourhood did laugh heartily with him who laughed because he had won. The ridiculousness of Griffith's position tickled everybody—he, for his own benefit, setting another man on to do a certain thing, and when the man had done it quarrelling with him, because he had done it too promptly!

But in the second week, he heard that persons whose judgment he valued, and whose favourable opinion was vital in commercial matters, began to treat the business more gravely.

In the third he went to his lawyer—the same who had brought the commission business to so happy a termination—and told him with characteristic simplicity and frankness what he had thought, and how far he had been disappointed. He ended with the question,

'Taking the thing as I have said, and using your individual knowledge and experience as a man of the world besides, I ask you if there is anything sufficiently dangerous to carackter to demand action? I stand on my carackter, Mr. North, and no man shall damage that while I have breath in my body, or a shilling in my pocket!'

Mr. North was aware from Israel's look, voice,

and manner, he meant not merely all he said, but more, when he used these last words. There was no anger in them, but there was deliberate thought and unchanging will.

Somehow Mr. North so much respected that will, and, so much feared it for Israel's own sake if it made any mistakes, that, from a kind of sympathy with him, he replied briefly,

'I understand. Come to me again at the end of a fortnight. We will both in the meantime observe and collect facts.'

Israel came at the time appointed—looking cheery—the lawyer fancied. He waited to hear what the latter had to say, who was hesitating, cautious, and on the whole inclined to let the affair blow over, as no doubt it would sooner or later.

'My experience and views are different,' was Israel's response. 'Here are notes of things said to certain folk, and here are the names of some of them who can be trusted to repeat what they heard in a court of justice. Proceed, and quickly. He's hurting me. What money will you want?'

It will be understood now on what business the two lawyers had again met.

And for what end? Why simply to repeat in substance the former conclusion.

Griffith's adviser, Mr. Spettigue, found it alike impossible to prove that Israel had done a single dishonest act, or to resist the proofs arrayed on the opposite side, that his client had become actionable for slander and injury to character; and that heavy damages would have to come out of his pocket, if the contest had to be fought in a court of justice.

It appeared in the discussion that Griffith had given warning to his lawyer, after several long and heated interviews, that he might yield if he liked once more; but that if he did so, it would be for the last time: he would never employ him again.

'So, you see,' remarked the lawyer, with a shrug, 'I must lose my client, or go to work to ruin him by a process of endless litigation.'

If all solicitors were like these two, the profession would indeed be as honoured as honourable. They really did listen to each other, and

strive to get at fair and hopeful conclusions for
both the men represented. And it made the fact
all the more remarkable that they were just the
two men whose interests were the most opposed.
They shared between them all the best business
of the district, and they lived and had their
offices just opposite each other, in the market
place of the principal town—Leath.

There was, however, it must be owned, at that
time, a faint whisper heard occasionally—nobody
knew by—or to—whom uttered, but suggesting
the idea of these gentlemen's partnership : an idea
which made each of the persons concerned so very
angry when it reached him through inquisitive
lips, that no one presumed again to touch upon it.

Meantime in their dealings with Griffith and
Israel, they fought stoutly, and yielded fairly, for
their respective clients, or would have done so
but that, as Mr. Spettigue observed, plaintively,

' My client gives me so little chance to ask you
to yield fairly ; he is once more hopelessly wrong.'

' Well, I will take no advantage of your
candour. I have as yet said nothing to Israel about
this, but I shall on my own responsibility waive all

claim for damages or costs if you, on behalf of Mr. Griffith Williams, consent to put into my hands a paper to the effect that, differences having arisen, and charges having been made, we have gone into the matter as friends, rather than as legal advisers of both these gentlemen, and have come to the conclusion that the charges are not substantiated, and are, therefore, withdrawn. This paper to be shown to any one we please, but not made public in any other way.'

'He must do that! He shall, or find somebody else to act for him.'

The paper was drawn up, a copy made, and away went Mr. Spettigue in one direction to find Griffith Williams, while Mr. North went off in the other to seek Israel.

It was noticeable, the conduct of the two men. Content with obtaining substantial redress, Israel signed at once without a word the paper put before him. Whereas Griffith Williams the moment he read the document tore it into a hundred pieces, and scattered them upon the wind, that it might carry them where it listed.

'There!' he said, looking unutterable things at

the faithless negotiator; and walked away without condescending a second word.

Just as Mr. Spettigue expected, he received in a few hours a note fawningly polite from one of the pettifoggers of the profession, desiring, at Mr. Griffith Williams' request, that all papers, securities, documents, and valuables of whatever kind he held, belonging to that gentleman, might be immediately forwarded to the writer, George Croft. He was invited also to enclose his account, which should be immediately settled.

'Ah!' said Mr. Spettigue, breathing a deep breath, 'the Squire's got the right man at last to run him at the devil's own pace down into the bottomless pit.'

CHAPTER IV.

CONFESSION OR DAMAGES?

ISRAEL heard with perfect equanimity of the failure of the proposal made on his behalf, and merely said to Mr. North,

'As I expected. Proceed!'

An action for slander was accordingly begun, and the damages were laid at a thousand pounds.

Mr. Croft was certain all would end rightly. It was a question of money only. Witnesses were expensive articles. This idea was hinted in a somewhat mysterious manner that made Mr. Griffith Williams uncomfortable, but when he asked questions it was explained away.

So matters proceeded to the day of trial : when an accidental conversation with an old Quaker friend, a Mr. Sturch, who happened to be tolerably familiar with the facts on both sides, so alarmed

the Squire about the antecedents of some of Mr.
Croft's witnesses, and for the aspect his own
character, as a supposed man of honour and a
magistrate, might be made to bear in the court,
that he agreed, if the compromise he had before
rejected were offered now, he would accept it. He
would himself propose nothing. Self-respect
forbade. He reminded his friend the costs were
now considerable, and these he supposed he must
pay.

His friend, the Quaker, warned him against
supposing he would get off so easily; and waiting
no reply went to seek Israel, who was in the
mine; pursuing his labours as though, in the comparison, actions-at-law and courts of justice were
hardly worth a thought.

The broad-brimmed friend was chivalrous
enough to go down to him to save time, though
sharing all Griffith Williams' disgust of the descent
and of that to which it led.

He found Israel too busy to speak to him for a few
minutes, and with hands and face blacker than anyone had ever seen him even in his Overman days.
If he was hard to David, he was at all events still

more obdurate to himself. Proprietor as he now
was he had been busily engaged for some hours
with picked men in the very delicate and dangerous operation of propping with new supports a
weak place in the roof, he himself foremost in the
labour and the risk through the whole operation.

'I think that'll do as a temporary thing, Lewis,'
he said, looking at the work, and then at the man
addressed.

'I wouldn't trust it for long. There'll be a Fall
here for certain, if you do.'

'We begin the general renovation in a week or
two, so if it'll only last till then—'

He noticed his Quaker friend's anxious face, but
before going to him he looked again at the work,
and then he and Lewis put up yet another prop.

And then he went to his visitor, declining to
shake hands, and holding up one hand in explanation to be seen, while with the other he lifted
the lamp. Mr. Sturch laughed ; then said,

'Have you any hostile feeling to gratify in this
trial ? '

Israel did not answer for quite half a minute.
No doubt he was taking in all the question

implied. He looked on the ground, and his face seemed to grow blacker than usual in the deep shade.

'No;' he said at last, lifting his clear steely eyes, which shone in the lamp-light, to the querist's face. 'Set my carackter fair before men, and I'm content.'

'You will make no money demands?'

'No, it would be unwise,' said Israel, deliberately. 'I shall gain most by taking least.'

'You are perfectly right,' said the Quaker, shaking Israel's hand warmly, and forgetting or disregarding how dirty it was. 'Those who were in doubt, will doubt you no longer, when they hear you are so moderate. I don't want to come down again. Where will you be in three or four hours?'

'I will follow you presently to the court.'

Mr. Sturch once more returned to Griffith, found him wavering, and on the whole inclined to let the trial go on. The case, he said, was expected to be called in a few minutes.

'Come with me,' said the Quaker, 'and I will show you something.'

He took him into the court, and they passed on

their way a number of men and women, with Mr.
Croft in their centre, busily engaged in conversation with one or two of the number.

'Look at these. They are your witnesses.'

Griffith did look, and could not but own he had
never seen a more villanous, disreputable-looking
set. Not a single decent person of known respectability could he recognise among them.

'These, I suppose, are to prove somehow or
other a deep-laid plot on Mort's part to swindle
you out of the mine—a conspiracy with only one
man to conspire. Now glance further ahead.
Note the way I look. You see that knot of
persons, known, nearly every man of them, to you
and to me as men of credit, and mostly men of
substance. These are Israel's witnesses. And consider, my friend, how easy a task they have—
merely to repeat what you have said to them,
what you still say if any temptation incites you to
speak. Let us go outside.'

Griffith was convinced, yielded, and signed the
document that was virtually, if pushed home
against him, a confession of slander; and that document lay henceforward in the hands of his detested
enemy.

CHAPTER V.

DAVID SEEKS ROSES, AND FINDS THORNS.

It need hardly be said that Griffith Williams hated Israel a thousand times worse than before, when he heard men praise his foe's behaviour as magnanimous—as Christian-like in letting the Squire off so easily.

From that moment his whole nature assumed new and darker tints. He thirsted for vengeance, and he thirsted the more because it seemed so far out of his reach.

An unexpected incident, while opening to his heated vision prospects of future trouble, gave him the opportunity he sought sooner than he had ventured to hope for it.

He was walking one Sunday afternoon in the little wood of Brynnant, believing he was seeking shade and shelter from the intense heat and oppressive

glare of the open sunshine, but in reality trying
to escape from the eyes of men, who seemed to
look on him so differently—with so little of the
old confidence and respect.   But the wood gave
him more than this.   At that hour it was deserted ;
and as his morbid thoughts found their only solace
in solitude, he could here freely give way to the
self-communion which had become a part of their
habitual life.

The world, whose beauty had been so dear to
him, had become hateful.   The very air seemed
impregnated with the darkness and odour and
foulness of that mine which now was in part
Israel's.   His baleful figure would at the touch
of a passing thought rise suddenly as from some
petty receptacle, and soar like the genius in
the ' Arabian Nights,' up, up, up, right up into
the skies, and become so vast in its proportions as
to shut out the very sight and feeling of the sun.

He had such a mood on him now, as he
wandered about between the tree trunks, seeking
rest, trying often for it by sitting down, but
finding none.

He was pondering over a question that had

often occurred of late. Was it not possible to
circumvent Israel yet? To beat him at his own
cunning game? To buy back the mine quite
unexpectedly, and then have the intense delight of
explaining everything politely—oh, most politely!
—to the beaten vagabond?

Griffith felt he could risk half his fortune to
accomplish such a result.

But how? There he felt baffled. Mrs. Jehoshaphat was too much delighted with her bargain to
be willing to sell. The mine was to her a gigantic
toy; a fund of infinite amusement, for the aged
woman's second but vigorous childhood; a vent
for her irrepressible spirit and wayward mental
energies; a solace for her decaying frame, her
bodily pains, and her enfeebled and almost useless limbs.

Besides, how, even if he could buy her out,
was Israel's share to be dealt with?

Angry with himself for yielding to these
delusive notions, which he felt to be utterly un-
real, he began to cut away furiously the luxuriant
tops of a fine crop of stinging nettles; and in so
doing stung himself, a fact he recognised with a

hearty curse on all things past, present, or future, divine or human.

At that moment his attention was arrested by a peculiar whistle, though why he noticed it he might have been puzzled to explain.

Presently it was repeated, and seemed to come nearer.

He could not help fancying it was a signal of some kind, and he grew curious to see if he was right. Anything, no matter how trivial, was welcome to him just then, for it drew his thoughts away from themes that did him, as he knew, nothing but injury.

A third time and still nearer was the same clear, penetrating, inquiring sound heard; and then as by way of answer came from behind him a prolonged cry in the shrillest and sweetest of fairy voices of ' Da-a-a-a-a-vid ! ' followed by ringing delicious laughter.

The blood rushed into Griffith's face, and suffused his very eyes, as he turned and saw his own darling little Nest with a basket of flowers advancing towards him who whistled, as if the signal was for her, and it was she who had answered it.

He stepped behind a bush, hoping she had not seen him, and, as he did so, saw a boy—no doubt David—advancing rapidly towards where Nest was.

As the lad came near, Griffith's jealous eyes could not but notice how well he looked. His mother had evidently got some special idea into her head about him ; for she had managed to get him a Sunday suit made so superior in point of taste and style to anything known in the village that the neighbours were sure she must have gone to Leath for it; and not to Leath only, but to Leath's most fashionable and expensive tailor.

Whether the lad felt, as boys will feel, elated by this novelty in his condition, or whether he saw it only through Nest's eyes, and, therefore, gloried in it ; or whether the idea of meeting her, added to the sense of the sweetness of the holy-day, and of the supreme beauty of the weather— whether any or all of these things together moved him or no, it is certain that his face was a picture of such glowing beauty and expectant delight, as he passed the bush, and met Nest, that Griffith Williams felt softened for a moment towards him, and almost envied Israel his pride in such a son.

Then recalling how he had seen David in the mine under such ignoble circumstances, he used the fact to illustrate the general badness of Israel's heart and character, and to stimulate all his hatred anew; and when once that feeling obtained full possession of him, all other and better feelings faded for the moment, even if they did not disappear altogether.

'Nest, you darling little thing, where have you been?' cried David. 'I have been whistling like a blackbird for you, I don't know how long.'

'Why you see, David, mamma said she was sorry she had promised to let me bring you some flowers. She was sure papa would be angry. And then I cried. And she wanted to pacify me by saying that some day things might be different, but now I mustn't mind; I must be good, and all that. But, David, I wasn't good, and so she let me come. But I must run away directly. And you mustn't go home with me.'

'Shan't I though, but I shall.'

He took the basket of flowers from her hand, and, after some minutes of pretty contention on both sides, they took hands, and were about to stroll away together, but not towards home.

No. David had found the first white wild roses of the year in bloom, and he must show her where, and make a garland for her.

Poor children! The change that came over their faces as they suddenly saw standing before them, at a turn of their path, the awful figure of Mr. Griffith Williams was such as might have moved the hardest heart, much less the heart of a man like the Squire, which was not naturally at all hard.

But he was in the early stage of a moral disease, when natural things become unnatural to the jaundiced eyes. One maddening thought alone now possessed him, that already his wife was preparing a scorpion's nest for him in his own future home; that she and doubtless Mrs. Mort were in accord, and had between them settled that David and his daughter—*his!*—were to be early initiated in the thought of a future alliance.

Well, he would settle that once for all; and meantime cursed the folly of his wife.

The children trembled as they saw his look,

and the riding-whip in his hand, but seemed unable to speak.

He strode towards them quietly enough, till he was able to place his hand on David's shoulder, and grasp it as in a vice.

' Put down those flowers,' he said.

' Please, sir,' said David, falteringly, but as loth to give up Nest's gift, ' she gave them to me.'

' Put them down,' thundered Griffith.

' Do, David, dear ! ' said the innocent Nest, but using words that were as oil to the fire in her father's breast.

A sudden lash was the only other warning given, followed by a scream from David, and another from Nest. And the father's passion once given way to, raged without check or remorse. Again and again, and yet again he struck the boy ; and no one could have guessed how long he might have gone on, but for the sight of his own child at his feet, clasping his knees, and exhibiting such distress in tears, sobs, and passionate outcries, that he at last paused, and threw away the whip, as he said to David,

' There, my lad ! Whenever, your whole life

through, you think again of my daughter, think of this and be wise.'

He then stooped, took Nest up in his arms, but found he had in those few moments virtually changed for her and himself all the sweet loving confidence both had so much prized.

She would say nothing to him. She dried her eyes in a little time, though it was a long while before the convulsive heavings of the little breast could also subside. She leaned upon his shoulder, but it was from exhaustion. He felt through his whole frame as if some new spirit of revulsion had been born out of all this anguish; and though he strove to justify himself to his own conscience, he seemed to be unable to listen to it—he heard only the silent pleadings of his little daughter against him—which seemed to go up to heaven.

Should he say something to David, whom he had not looked at since the violence done him? After all the boy was but a boy, and had doubtless been put up to this by the arts of a low mother, and by the subtle ambition of a wicked father.

When he did turn to see what the boy was doing, he found David had gone away.

To carry the story home, of course! Israel's son, the new manager and mine-owner's son, had been horsewhipped. Here was new material for the gossips.

Somehow Griffith felt sick. Do what he would, his thoughts would go to the helpless boy—not to the boy's father, for whose sake the violence had been committed.

His wife! What would she say? She had better say nothing. Why, after all, it was to her senseless folly the outrage—if it was one—was due.

Whatever comfort this circumstance was calculated to give, failed, however, to convince Griffith Williams he had not done a most barbarous act; and he went home more profoundly humiliated, more deplorably wretched than he had ever before been in his whole life.

That day he felt would make its mark upon him for evermore.

CHAPTER VI.

HOW DAVID PLAYED THE SPARTAN BOY.

FOR some days Griffith Williams was left in a curious state of suspense, hourly expecting to see Israel again clamorous, about the outrage on David; or else some legal or other messenger from him, probably bringing a summons to appear before a brother magistrate.

They were by no means enviable days with such a prospect before him of new troubles, more bitter personal humiliations. Besides, he found it impossible to shut out the fact that matters were, as a whole, growing worse and worse. The tone of his daily life was becoming embittered, his self-respect consciously lessening. Yet, instead of being thereby warned to stop, he felt impelled more vehemently than ever to go on till he had routed and eternally disgraced this mean yet dangerous enemy. And then—why then, perhaps, he might forgive and forget in time, and let the peace of oblivion and contempt reign betwixt them.

Colouring these thoughts with its own peculiar sinister light came every now and then over them the idea that Israel's prolonged silence about the horsewhipping might mean fresh plots, more serious dangers. It was quite out of the question that he could intend to be silent, and to let such a thing pass. What, then, was he—what could he be contemplating?

But the remarkable part of the affair was that nobody seemed to know anything about the incident beyond the limits of his own household, and there it was only known to Nest and her mother.

He never took up a local newspaper but he expected to see a paragraph with some sensational heading, and in the middle of it his own and Israel Mort's names in portentous capital letters. But the Press seemed as indifferent to David's horsewhipping as all the rest of the world; unless, indeed, out of respect to him they were determined to be silent till compelled to speak as a matter of ordinary duty.

It never occurred to him till an entire week had gone to ask whether it was probable or possible that the boy had kept the affair secret.

Griffith had not credited him with so much good sense, as that of desiring to conceal so disgraceful a punishment. But at last he began seriously to believe the fact was so, and his opinion of David sensibly changed and improved.

The lad, he thought, must have the courage of a pretty strong self-control, if he could help telling those who would so surely have sympathised with him. And as usual with Griffith, when compelled to think better of those he quarrelled with, he was also compelled to think worse of himself. As David's behaviour grew less criminal in his eyes, the punishment he had inflicted became less satisfactory to him who had been at once witness, jury, judge, and executioner, and the implied disgrace at times almost threatened to recoil on its author.

He was sorry he had allowed himself to be tempted into violence. Still it might do the boy good. If he didn't mistake, there was a touch of his father's obstinacy visible through all the timidity and gentleness of his behaviour when he hesitated so about putting down the flowers. So all might be for the best. The incident might warn him against experiments at a later time, when he could neither get off so easily as regards punishment, nor be able with so little effort to disentangle his own misplaced affections. That lad, as a man, would be a dangerous lover. Happily Griffith was warned. And so was David.

And then the matter gradually died out of his mind.

But not so out of the minds of others. David had not told Israel, but resolved even in the most cruel anguish of his hurts he never should be told. But his heart failed him of its purpose to conceal the matter also from his mother. He opened the door, biting his lips to keep his mouth shut. But as he shut the door and went in, nature became paramount, and the intended secret burst forth amid a passion of tears, his face crimson and dark with shame.

The mother's first impulse was to rush out and seek the assailant. And when David, seeing her so moved, quieted her by quieting himself, even then the poor, spiritless, broken-down woman was stirred to such new life by the sight of the livid purple weals across her boy's loins as she undressed him, and applied some soothing lotion to the sores, that she wanted to go and seek Israel, and not even wait for his return at the ordinary hour.

David soon convinced her that for everybody's sake it would be best to say nothing. Nest would like that, he was sure. So would Mrs. Griffith, who was always very kind to him. And as to himself, the idea of the public knowing what had happened, was too dreadful even to be thought of.

'I am a great coward, mother,' said David. 'I shrieked when he first struck me, but I do think I could let him lash me again, very badly, if only he promised to tell no one. It was Nest's being there that hurt me most. And that,' said the boy, with sudden violence—and yet with tears streaming down his cheeks—'that I'll never forgive him, never!'

As to Israel, they could take no counsel from him. Both instinctively shrank in horror from the mere thought. They knew well that, however little he might be able to sympathise with David's sufferings and sensitiveness, he would feel

that the greatest possible outrage had been committed upon him—Israel himself, and that the
measures he might take in consequence would
destroy every chance of future reconciliation.

While David was yet shrinking with the acute
pain at every touch of his mother's careful, but
not exactly skilful hand, there came a soft knock
at the door.

'Cover me up, mother. Oh, don't, don't let
anybody see or know!'

David did not for the moment feel sure that it
was not Nest outside.

While Mrs. Mort hastily strove to obey him,
the door was gently opened; and, to the astonishment of both, Mrs. Griffith Williams stood on the
threshold.

David was too far undressed to be able to follow
his first impulse—to run away upstairs; so he
drew around him hurriedly and shamefacedly the
garment nearest to his hand—his little jacket—but
his mother pulled it away, and courtesying with a
strange mingling of respect and defiance, and her
pale face visibly reddening, said, as she pointed to
David's back,

'Oh, please come in, ma'am, and see your husband's doings! Look at him! Look at my boy's back!' And therewith she began to cry.

'Oh, my dear good David!' cried out, with impetuous heart, the Squire's wife; as she put her arms round him and kissed him, remaining quite unaware of the torture she was inflicting on David; while he, coward as he said he was, bore these pangs heroically, and smiled, as he in response clasped his arms round her neck, and kissed her, and said,

'Oh, it don't matter! Please tell Nest I don't care a bit about it now—no, not a bit!'

Mrs. Griffith Williams again kissed him, and said,

'I could not rest till I had seen you and your mother, and told you how grieved I am, and how wretched my little darling is. In fact, to tell the truth, it is she has almost driven me here, unknown to her father. She's such a sensitive child, Mrs. Mort. I'm often afraid I shall never rear her. She's quite ill now, and her father is in much trouble about her, and many things besides. But there, I mustn't begin talking—about things, too, that he says I don't understand.

But that's nonsense! For if one doesn't understand at my age, I wonder when I shall! I must
run back now. I wouldn't for the world have
Griffith know I am out.'

She had left David's side a little, but returned
now, and whispered to him,

'My darling was so hurt about the flowers, that
I promised to bring you one. There it is, a
yellow rose. Now kiss me. Good-bye. Good-
bye, Mrs. Mort. Only a little secret betwixt
David and me. You are to ask no questions,
mind.'

Mrs. Mort could only respond in a similar spirit.
And with mutual expressions of hope in some
future and brighter day to come, when something
good might happen, the nature of which neither
appeared to like to speak of, or in any way to
define, they separated.

As to David, vain indeed would be the attempt
to picture his delight as he held Nest's gift—the
beauteous rose—in his fingers, and smelt it, and
turned it round, and studied it in every possible
aspect, and wondered if there ever had been such
a flower in existence before.

But now arose a new difficulty. The boy was obviously unfit to go to work next morning. Yet how tell Israel so? David's whole system was shaken. He needed rest, freedom from aught that might still further inflame his sores, and constant attention to alleviate them. The mine was just about the very worst place in the whole world the lad could go to under such circumstances; and the mere thought of David's working in it, with all its inevitable bodily difficulties of motion—its stoopings, and crawlings, and unnatural postures, made his mother shiver, and cry out,

'No, David, that mustn't be thought of! But then what shall be said to your father? If I tell him you are unwell, and think of some naturally sufficient excuse, he won't take my word for it, nor will he rest till he has found us out; and then he'll say we are deceiving him, and be very hard on us.'

David thought, and winced, and thought again, and once more winced; then remembered his rose, which had been already deposited in a slender phial filled with water, and placed within his reach. He smelt at that, and made up his mind.

'I shall go to the mine to-morrow, mother.'

'No, no, David.'

'Mother, I shall go.'

And he went.

In one aspect of the matter it was a pity Israel did not, at the close of that trying day for poor David, know the truth ; for to a certainty he would have been moved, and perhaps for the first time in his life, into active sympathy with and better understanding of his son. For here one of Israel's little secrets may be let out. It was, then, one of his objects, in dealing so sternly with David, to wring out of him those weak elements in his character which with Israel were such objects of contempt ; namely, the lad's sensitiveness and gentleness, which had something feminine in them, and the ulterior uses or value of which Israel knew nothing, guessed nothing.

CHAPTER VII.

MRS. JEHOSHAPHAT'S CORDIAL.

THERE was one person who wonderfully enjoyed these differences between Israel and his former employer—however unpleasant they might be to the parties themselves—and that was Mrs. Jehoshaphat.

It was as good as a play, she more than once told the former, to have him come and sit by her bed-side, and narrate every incident, however slight, and as far as possible repeat every word that had been said.

He had to show his wound—for Israel had hurt his hand against the dog's teeth, through the force of the blow; he had to repeat what this lawyer had said, and what that one had answered. He had to tell how Griffith looked at certain critical moments, and how the two men faced one another when they next met, and so on.

And then came the trophies of the double victory. She exulted at the sight of the cheque for 750*l*., which she made him bring for her to see before he opened his account with it at the Leath Bank. She was still more deeply gratified when, at a later day, she read the memorandum Griffith Williams had been obliged to give, unsaying all his bitter charges that he had cast broadside through the neighbourhood.

'I say, Israel Mort,' she almost shouted out to him, after the perusal of this document, her eyes gleaming with humour and delight, ' you are a very dangerous man to have dealings with! Very. I don't think I am quite safe. Do you? You have done me once, you know, and in the same transaction that has put out our friend the Squire so much. Perhaps I ought to have joined with him in the attack on you. Assailed at once in the van and the rear, and on both flanks, where would you have been? Eh?'

'I ain't time, ma'am,' was Israel's response, 'for fighting with imaginary difficulties. It's hard work enough, I assure you, to deal with the real ones— I mean the mine, which is in an awful state. How

Mr. Jehoshaphat managed to sleep at nights for thinking of it, passes me.'

'Why shouldn't he? You slept of nights, didn't you? and you were always in far greater danger than he, who seldom went below. He was too good a judge!'

'Miners, ma'am, carry their lives in their hands so long, they forget at last they have 'em there. But the property at stake, that's what he cared for, and what I was thinking of. I suppose, however, he had extracted so much from the pit during his long term, that he could at last feel content, whatever happened. Let the mine blow up, or let the water burst in, it didn't matter to him. Mr. Jehoshaphat had taken jolly good care for himself.'

'I'm afraid you are right, Israel. And now that Mr. Jehoshaphat's dynasty is no more, and that Mrs. Jehoshaphat's and Mr. Israel Mort's begins, how are things going on?'

'We ain't done much yet. There's so much to prepare first. Making contracts, collecting workmen from different parts, getting materials together. I am buying the materials all at the cheapest markets. I reckon to save some hundreds in that item alone, over and above what your husband used to pay.'

'You do! Well, if you beat him in anything, there's only one other person for you to beat.'

'You, ma'am?'

'I! Good lord, no! The evil one!'

The implied compliment, however, did not escape the lady, whose genial spirits almost began to infect Israel.

'You are very busy, then, at the mine even now?' she asked.

'Busy! Come and have a look at it. I wish you would.'

'Israel, man, that's the one thing on earth just now I seem to care for. But the doctor says, "No, I sha'nt." He's a horrible despot; and, as to language, pays me, I suppose, in my own coin. Says it might be dangerous. I can't tell. He's always croaking about my being so careless. Careless!—after I have let him shut me up here, like a mouse in a trap, in this one room, for I don't know how many weeks!'

'Do your mind good, ma'am, to go, and that often is the way to do good to the body!'

'Don't say anything to him or anybody else, but tell me, how it can be managed? Quick! tell me!'

The difficulty was this: Mrs. Jehoshaphat had now removed, with such of her curiosities as she could take with her, to her late husband's residence, which was perched like an eagle's nest on the edge of a precipitous height that overlooked a magnificent expanse of sea, marshy plain, and mountainous range: a prospect she was quite able to appreciate. From the windows she could see the mine—about half-a-mile distant—and the inaccessibility of the residence mattered nothing to one who had no lady visitors, and who rarely went out.

'How did you get up here?' asked Israel.

'By a carriage, with stones stuck under the wheel at every yard or two of the worst places, to prevent slipping back. But I'll never trust myself so again. The steep was frightful!'

'Well, ma'am, suppose a chair were got from the town. I'd find a couple of men who'd draw you

nicely, and where they couldn't draw you would
carry you as softly and as safely as if you were a
new-born babe.'

'Ha, ha, ha! That's what I fear I am—at
least, what I'm coming to, having already reached
my second childhood. But what's the value of
life if you don't enjoy it? Give me now only
three years stuffed full, daily, of interesting
things to see, to hear of, or to talk about; let
me know the mine is repaired and at full work—
hundreds of people earning a good living for
themselves, and making lots of money for us—let
me see all that, Israel, and you doing me credit
for trusting you—ah! let me have that—and I'll
ask no more.' So spake Mrs. Jehoshaphat; and
at the conclusion smacked her lips, as with enjoyment of the taste left on them by her words.

She had risen in bed from her recumbent
posture, while her eyes were glowing with wild
excitement, and her grey hair in tangled masses
was falling about her withered neck, and over
her half uncovered breast.

Presently she became conscious of this personal
disorder, covered herself, and leaned back; and

said with an air of sudden lassitude that contrasted
painfully with what Israel had witnessed just
before,

' When shall I come? '

' We will have all ready for you on Thursday
next.   The chair and the men shall be with you
about eleven in the morning.   I'd advise you to
bring plenty of wraps, though the weather is
warm, and a good stout cordial in a bottle.'

' Perhaps, perhaps !   The cordial for me,
Israel, is to see a man at work like you.   A
real man !   There ! be off, or you'll fancy I'm
waiting for the death of Mrs. Mort to ask you to
marry me.'

A burst of laughter, soon changed into a cough,
then again a fresh burst of mirth, were the last
sounds Israel heard as he left his eccentric mis-
tress.

CHAPTER VIII.

A FAILURE CONFESSED.

ISRAEL was in all the bustle of the new works when one day there appeared before him the figure of a man he had often thought of since the day of their separation with some regret, but more of annoyance.

Rees Thomas walked into the office looking so thin and physically wretched, yet with such a light in his eye—as though that saw something unseen by others—and with so much of simple unaffected dignity in his bearing, that Israel was interested in spite of himself and the resentment he felt and waited to show, if need be.

'I have been very unfortunate, Mr. Mort,' he began, 'since I left you.'

He paused, and Israel got up and placed a chair for him, and bade him sit down; then waited in silence, checking the reply that sprang to his lips asking, Why, then, hadn't he had more sense, and have stayed where he was?

'Employers, to be candid, seem not only to share your objections, Mr. Mort, about the morning prayers, but to object to me besides for only having proposed such things.'

'Did you tell them, then?' asked Israel.

'Certainly. I could do no other while seeking the post of Deputy or Overman.'

'You mean you would not waive for them that which you refused to me?'

'Yes.'

'Well, that's right, Rees Thomas; that's right.'

'Failing as Deputy or Overman, they, for the reason I have given, refused even to employ me as a simple collier! The word seems to have been passed round that I am dangerous, because I try to do a little good in my own humble way as a follower of Christ.'

'You mean in mere talk between man and man, as opportunity serves, not collecting them formally together and interrupting labour?'

'Yes.'

'Fools! I don't object to that. Though I fear many of my men would fancy they had got a scapegoat in you to carry off all their sins, and so sin away harder than ever.'

Israel laughed, but, seeing his hearer did not, immediately relapsed into his ordinary iron-clad sort of visage.

'Will you, then, employ me as a simple collier?' said Rees Thomas, after a pause of sadness produced by Israel's jest.

'Is not the work too hard for you? You are not naturally robust, and have been long an under-officer; and I fear that for you to return to the continuous and monotonous labour of coal-cutting —— '

'Let me try,' interrupted Rees Thomas earnestly. 'I will earn my wages, or go without them.'

'So be it.'

'I am sincerely indebted to you, Mr. Mort. God only knows what I should have done had you rejected me. I am at the lowest stage at which Fortune can place a man; another step, and I must have fallen into the abyss.'

'Your mind is unchanged as to the offer I before

made you? I could yet make an opening as Deputy at thirty shillings a week, and valuable perquisites.'

'It is kind of you to ask me, it is magnanimous, but it is you who must change in that, not me.'

'Go, then. Begin as soon as you like,' said Israel, roughly, and turned away to continue his previous avocation.

CHAPTER IX.

REES THOMAS IN A NEW LIGHT.

THOUGH of so demonstrative a nature in all that concerned his mission (for Rees Thomas, while one of the humblest of men, believed he had a mission), in all other matters he was shy, reticent, and inclined to glide shadow-like through the world, with as little of notice as possible. He was especially unwilling at all times to speak of himself, his troubles, or his poverty.

None, therefore, knew, and few even could suspect a circumstance that gave ten-fold intensity to what he was now suffering on account of his poverty and physical weakness. He was in love, and beloved by one of the most attractive of women in that class of which alone he had any personal experience.

Margaret Doubleday was the daughter of the

old woman with whom Rees Thomas had lodged for many years, except when temporarily away from the neighbourhood. These two had comforted him at the very beginning of their acquaintance by giving him a home when he was out of employment, sharing with him their exceedingly limited means, till Fortune smiled again, and work and wages were renewed once more.

Then Rees Thomas brought them week after week every sixpence he earned, leaving himself nothing for those little indulgences which we all so much covet; and even going without fresh and warmer clothing that the season made necessary, in his determination to pay his debt to them without a moment's avoidable delay.

That matter, however, they then took into their own hands, and placed one evening ready for him on his chair, when he should sit down to the evening meal, a thick warm overcoat of the precise kind he needed and liked.

The tears came into his eyes when he saw what they had done; and, for a wonder, he did not reproach them, as they expected, with the reminder of how much he yet owed them. He put it on

before them, felt it, examined the pockets, stowed
away in them all his small tools and conveniences
of various kinds that he, like all thoughtful miners,
carried ; then looked at himself in the glass with
such evident satisfaction, and patted his sides so
complacently, that the delighted women hardly
knew whether to laugh or cry, so did both at once.

From that hour perhaps might be dated the
beginning of the love affair.

Margaret had previously seen in Rees Thomas
only two aspects, that of the serious, sad, not to
say depressed workman ; and that of the energetic
minister of Christ—his mind full of vivid religious
light, his heart brimming over with religious
tenderness, but the lofty tenderness of his Divine
Master, which never forgot in its care for humanity
what it was aiming to accomplish.

She had felt with him, as we have seen, in the
one aspect, but only as a sister might feel ; she
admired, venerated, feared him in the other ; so
deeply indeed that to think of loving him, or of
imagining he could descend from such spiritual
heights to think of her in any other way than as a
disciple, was quite beyond her.

Rees Thomas, on his part, with his thoughts habitually pre-occupied by the intense desire to do some good, however humble—for he was a man of no personal ambition, seemed to lack indeed some useful quality in that direction—never thought of her but as one towards whom he owed whatever of grateful brotherly affection and of spiritual 'suit and service' he could render.

And if he had thought of her for an instant as a possible wife for him, he had certainly shrunk back in dismay at his own egotism and folly. What!—she, young, strikingly engaging in her person and manners—sure, therefore, to have offers from men enjoying all those advantages of person and pecuniary position that he lacked—she marry him, the poor collier; for he was not even then a Deputy! Absurd! Wrong even to think of. He would take care he would think of it no more.

And he kept to his purpose for a little while, until this incident of the coat took place; which, trivial in itself, revealed him to her in just that aspect of simple genial humanity, which alone she needed to encourage and stimulate her liking into a warmer sentiment.

From that moment a change went on almost unconsciously to both. She would venture to ask him questions on sublunary topics, to tell him of matters that had interested her in the people, or things about her, and find to her gratification that he, instead of regarding her talk as trifling, responded with similar but richer experiences from his own daily life; and became quite animated in such discourse, while delighting her with his touches of character, and his keen perceptions of their humorous side, to which she had fancied him inaccessible.

Then, too, she found how richly his mind was stored with just the knowledge she had fancied him most destitute of, the practical things of daily life.

She found, too, that his tastes and natural habits all led in exactly the direction to which she had fancied he was most opposed—home and domestic comfort. That very smallest of worlds—the family—was exactly the one world wherein all his merely personal desires and ambition were limited.

He brought books home and read to her. And

these were so judiciously selected, so adapted to her unliterary experience, that while they never wearied her, they always left behind in her remembrance some seeds of culture that promised in time an unexpected harvest.

Still neither for a moment thought of love.

Now it sometimes happens that love is wayward enough to prefer such a state of things, and to grow only the faster and more robust in consequence; either because it is thus left alone to its own natural impulses and laws, free from a thousand conventional taints and restraints, or because it gets a certain sly enjoyment out of the sight of two people pretending each to be moving in a certain direction, the one opposed to the other, whereas all the while they can't move a hair's breadth from the line that is leading fast to the fatal goal where they are to be shorn as with the scissors of the weird sisters of their single threads of life, and receive, instead, a double and mingled strand.

But discovery came at last. And discovery itself is at once the greatest charm of love, and the most powerful of influences in stimulating it to new zest, ardour, and strength.

So was it with Rees Thomas and Margaret.

The maiden was simply confused, but very happy at the discovery.

The man felt happy, too—so happy that it seemed wrong; and then he took that as a warning that he was forgetting the dearest aim of his life, his most sacred duty, and began to withdraw himself.

Thus for some little time the atmosphere of their humble dwelling was one full of the strangest lights and shades; faithfully reflecting the hopes and fears, the conflicts of duty with passion, that possessed the hearts and minds of the two actors therein.

And it was just at this critical period that Rees Thomas thought to solve the very serious problem presented to him by a kind of compromise shaped out in his own secret thoughts, to the effect that, before he spoke to Margaret, and so, perhaps, committed them both to what could not be again undone, he would feel he had achieved something for his Divine Master, that might excuse, if not justify, his worldly falling off.

Hence his determined efforts to establish prayers

in the mine as the fit preliminary to such daily work; hence his quarrel with Israel, his separation from him, his efforts to carry out his aims elsewhere, his utter and melancholy failure, and final return to drink the cup of anguish, disappointment, and humiliation to the very dregs by resigning Margaret, and once more casting in his lot with Israel.

He did resign her, and in so stern a manner— one she had not conceived it in his power to use —that poor Margaret, scarcely able to keep back her tears, yet felt called upon to display her womanly pride ; and when her mother strove to speak to her about the business, answered her with a quite unusual asperity and irritation.

And so all three were silenced.

CHAPTER X.

A FALL, AND ITS CONSEQUENCES.

REES THOMAS has been some days at work; and Margaret sees that on each recurring eve he comes back more weary than ever, faintly smiling away questions about himself, refusing offers to help, and retiring as soon as possible, after his meal, to the solitude, though not the rest, of his bed-chamber.

There is no more pleasant gossip now between them, no more reading, and Margaret finds life hard to bear, and is inclined bitterly to ask why he could not have left her alone before awakening in her such new hopes and aspirations, rather than after.

Still he goes on with the labour that is killing him. Let us follow him on a day that was to bring him face to face with yet a new aspect of destiny.

He was at work in a stall that opened from the engine-plane, or incline, monotonously hewing away, and almost as monotonously repeating what had become a sort of hourly formula of utterance with him.

'No ; men like me have no business to wed !'

The morning had been chilly, and the face of the coal where he was working not being very far from the shaft-bottom, he felt little of the high temperature that affects the industry of the miners in the deeper recesses of the pit. He had, therefore, retained his jacket.

Feeling warmer now, he rose to take it off, and was placing it on the top of a wall, when he became aware of a sudden check in the wind-draught.

This is always a more or less alarming circumstance, as it may mean a great Fall somewhere, that has interrupted the ventilation, and which may soon be followed by explosions, through the gas accumulating where it should have been dispersed and carried away ; or it may mean that the greater danger of an explosion has happened.

He could not even guess at the precise point

where the check occurred, nor at the magnitude of the affair.

A man working as much as a mile away may know of even a slight explosion, through such a check to the wind, if he be in the same current.

While he stood listening in suspense and fear, not so much for himself as for others, the colliers who had been working near drew towards him, as if with an instinctive faith in his mining knowledge, whatever they might think of him as a spiritual comforter, if danger or death were nigh.

'It is a Fall!' cried one. 'I knew it must come! I knew it months ago!'

'No,' said a second; 'it's an explosion, and we shall soon be meeting the choke-damp! Hadn't we better run?'

'Let us first see which way to run,' answered Rees Thomas, 'lest we run into the danger we wish to escape.'

'I know what it is,' said still a third; 'it's an inundation. The waters are breaking in upon us, and have filled up the seven foot dip, so that no air gets that way.'

A man came running towards them, and shouting as he ran, 'The roof has fallen in the No. Five level, and there's been an explosion since, and more are expected. Run for your lives!'

He turned, and they were all about to follow him, holding their lamps so as to give them all possible aid, when before they had advanced many yards, the lights grew dim, their breathing difficult, and they all as by one impulse stopped.

'We must go back,' called out Rees Thomas. 'Be calm, dear brethren, and all shall be well!'

Returning to the place where they were before, Rees Thomas snatched at his jacket, in which he had things that might prove of infinite value if wanted. He called to them to follow him.

He forgot now he was a simple collier, and he spoke with all the decision of one in authority.

Presently they reached in safety the main drift, where the air was still passable, and where they were in assured safety for the time.

But reflection came with all its bitterness. They had gone further away than they were before from the bottom of the shaft; and they knew there was a double barrier betwixt them and that place

of safety and deliverance, the Fall, and the un-
breathable air.

But Rees Thomas's soul was full of anxious inquiry as to the fate of the many men who were
at work in different parts of the pit.

He thought of individual persons, with whom he
had had sweet religious communion; he thought
of others who had sorely tried him by their ribald
jests and hostility to his every effort among their
companions, and he hardly knew as to which
class he felt more anxious to learn if they had
escaped; or if that darkness, to which the darkness of the mine is as nought, had come over
them, and set their spirits free to join in hope or
fear their Maker and Judge.

It was with the sense of receiving a great shock
that he thought just then of David.

But if he needed any more powerful incentives
than he already had, the thoughts of the lad, and
his danger, and of the possibility of saving him,
gave them to him.

They now heard groans, and a cry, and Rees
Thomas advanced as far as he dared in the
direction of the sound. Presently he returned

with a collier, who had crawled from the Fall through the darkness and the foul air, his lamp smashed and useless, and his arm broken.

He had been on their side of the Fall, and, happily so far for him, only just on its outskirts.

He feared, he said, that many men had been injured, and that more had perished.

Time passed, though none could tell how fast or how slow.

It seemed after a while to Rees Thomas that the mass of fallen matter that choked the way must have been penetrated by the manual efforts of people on the other side of the Fall, between it and the shaft, or else that the Fall itself had not yet come to its natural end, and that anyhow fresh air was beginning to pass through.

Inexpressible was the comfort this thought and belief gave to the imprisoned men.

Still in spite of repeated efforts they found it impracticable to reach the Fall by the proper route, and it became a question whether they should not try another, a circuitous one.

But that, objected one of the colliers, would, he

thought, carry them where the explosion had been.

'All the better,' responded Rees Thomas; 'if only we *can* go that way, for then we may find some of our men needing succour.'

So they went. There were seven of the party in all. They soon came upon the first tokens of the battle-field. Doors, trams, roadways in a state of utter wreck.

But they could go no further for the choke-damp, and the men were about to lie down, feeling at once despondent and inclined to sleep.

But Rees Thomas roused them with a voice like a clarion.

They must put up canvas doors to guide the wind, and the ventilation would be restored at once.

One collier, the most willing and able of the set, ran to fetch canvas, which lay at no great distance ready cut in squares.

Others collected tools, and made such preparations as they could. In half an hour the wind was got right.

Again they advanced, and were soon met by a

party, who, having no lights, but seeing the lights of
the others, called aloud.   Rees Thomas answered
also aloud :—

'Do I hear James Lusty's voice ?'

'Ay, ay, Rees Thomas ; ahl right, wind and
limb !'

'And the men with you ?'

'Ahl right too.'

'How many ?'

'Thirteen ?'

'God be praised !' was the silent ejaculation of
the collier-minister, as he reckoned the number
of the two batches together now known to be
safe.

By this time they had met; and as the first gang
held up their lamps to look at the new-comers, they
saw they had been struggling through water, that
their faces and hands were bleeding, and their
clothing and entire aspect showing the ordeal they
must have passed through.

Lusty was faint, in spite of his being so cheery,
and he insisted upon sitting down to drink the
cordial draught of tea Rees Thomas poured out
for him into a little leathern cup he carried.

The latter knew well had he given Lusty the can he would have drained the whole to the bottom, regardless of the wants of others.

While they rested, the story of Lusty and his party was told by one and another in interjections, with pauses between.

One man had heard a sound of explosion, but guessed it to be only a shot fired.

But Lusty himself heard nothing, guessed nothing, till going his round he met the sulphur. He ran from it, back to the men and warned them. Then they stayed still till the sulphur again reached them, and they had once more to fly, and pass in their way through the dip, where they lost their lamps, and were knocked about sadly in the darkness and in the water.

Rees Thomas wanted now to be moving, but he was in the presence of one who would brook n inroad on his authority. Lusty was not simply a Deputy now, but Overman.

Could he be persuaded in any way to abdicate for a while?—Rees Thomas wondered to himself.

He saw Lusty was no longer master of his own

mind and will, and he understood but too plainly it was through no fault of his own.

All the well-known effects of the air in that state known as choke-damp were upon him. His craving to lie down, his failing power of limb, the fading away of everything like energy or will —from all these he was suffering; and though he more than once responded to Rees Thomas's impassioned appeal to him to exert himself, to struggle—for that he would probably die if he did not, the effort was feeble, and came to nothing, and he slept.

The next half hour was the saddest of the day, and precisely because attended by no incident, because there was nothing to do but to suffer, to fear the worst, and to wait in cruel suspense.

One by one the lights of the lamps began to give out.

'Well,' said a voice, after a long and deep pause and heavy silence, 'I'm glad of one thing, whatever happens!'

'What's that?' asked Rees Thomas, not un-willing to have the awful stillness broken.

'That you, Rees Thomas, persuaded me to join

a benefit society, and my poor wife and children will have a decent sum to help 'em on, if this is to be the last of me!'

A heart-breaking groan burst from another collier, revealing without words what he who uttered it felt, as knowing that his dear ones were left without any such provision.

Rees Thomas thought the time had come to pray, and he told them so, saying they would understand why he had delayed, that they might not think they were to be praying when they should be working.

There were emphatic responses from many, and silence on the part of the rest.

Rees Thomas then offered up a fervent but short prayer of thankfulness, that so many precious lives had been spared, and of entreaty that all the rest might yet be gathered together safely.

But he knew well how much reason there was to expect that some, perhaps many lives had been, or would be lost; and, like a man who could be prudent even in his most fervent passion, he took care to say, and with deep significance of tone, that it was not their will, but God's that was to be done.

A deep hum of Amens comforted him with the assurance he had comforted them.

Lusty now awoke, and his words and entire behaviour showed he was suffering from hallucination of mind. He rose to his feet, looked sternly about him, and began to abuse all and sundry, for coming so late to work; and to give vent to oaths so brutal and revolting, as in his sane and wakeful hours would have shocked even himself, little sensitive as he was to such things, could he have heard them repeated.

Rees Thomas was glad when he again lay down and slept.

Seeing no particular and pressing danger to him, Rees Thomas decided to leave him there awhile, and try if he could yet find more of the inmates of the mine.

'David! David! David!' again he exclaimed to himself as he felt how all this delay might endanger him.

A fancy strangely superstitious for such a man came over him. Israel's luck had of late become a proverb in the village. Was it now to be his luck that events so serious as a great Fall, and one or more explosions after, should happen and yet not a single life be lost?

He was constantly reminding himself 'None yet. All safe as yet. Oh, that it may prove so as we go on!'

The mere fancy, with all that it involved, seemed to act like a prophecy, and to give new strength to his failing limbs.

So again the party, now a large one, advanced; Rees Thomas in the van as before.

Some objects attract him as he approaches them in the darkness. He holds up his lamp and sees a tram overturned and lying on its side. He shifts his lamp, and the light falls on a man's recumbent figure, then on his face, which is scanned eagerly by Rees Thomas.

He stoops and feels his pulse, he holds his cheek to the lips; alas! no blood is beating in the one, no breath oozing from the other. The man is dead. And as that man had been engaged, so in all probability Rees Thomas might have been engaged, had he not resigned his post, and gone away, and now returned in a humbler capacity; for it was his successor as Deputy that he looked upon.

He knelt down by the dead body, and prayed inaudibly for a few seconds. What of gratitude and praise he thought or did not think, none of his fellows heard then or afterwards.

That man had been one of the very bitterest of his opponents regarding the morning prayers, and had been chosen by Israel precisely for that reason.

When Rees Thomas's companions knew who it was that lay there, the first man known to be dead, perhaps also the last, there ran through the group low murmuring talk, that told but too plainly how much the new Deputy had been disliked; and how inclined they were in their present mood to look upon his fate as a judgment, that he of all men should have been willing to fill the former Deputy's place.

Had the question of morning prayers been put to the men on this melancholy occasion, when they were following their present leader and former Deputy through a veritable valley, not of the shadow of death, but of death itself, doubtless there would have been a unanimous and earnest call for their resumption.

As they were again advancing—Rees Thomas feeling every instant as though he heard, not in his actual ears, but through his soul, the pleading voice of David crying, ' Oh save me ! save me ! '— they were joined by two more men and two boys ; the latter revealing a tale of horror in their hands as they held them up to the light of the one lamp that alone remained burning, and showed their fingers bleeding and denuded of flesh. And yet the fact that they were saved so far—had yet a chance for dear life, inspirited them to make light of their own sufferings, and almost to smile and draw brave comfort from the look of sympathy they saw in Rees Thomas's countenance.

But when he heard their touching story, his sympathy changed into admiration of the courage and fortitude that had brought them through so great a peril.

They had nearly finished a job of repairing that had taken a long time to accomplish, and were getting so weary that one of the men had said to the other,

' Well, Tom, I'm going,' and he began to collect and put on his clothes.

' No, let's finish while we are at it,' urged the other.

Something warned the man (so he afterwards said) who had wanted to go, that he ought to stick to his purpose, but not liking to upset his comrade, he agreed to stay.

They had finished at last, and one of the two boys who had been waiting on them snatched up his clothes, and started off running; delighted, boy-like, to think he would soon be out of the pit, have his supper, and then join in a game of cricket.

Presently, while the others were preparing to follow him, they heard him cry out in sudden alarm.

Before they could get to him he came back running, and his clothes streaming down with water, to say the water was in the ' dip,' and he had got into it before he knew, and his foot slipped, and so he had gone down into it over head.

The two men looked at each other for a moment in blank stupor and silence.

Then one of them sat down on the ground, saying,

'We are done now! we are dead men!' and seemed ready to resign all hope and effort in the blackness of his despair.

'Come, Jim,' says the other, 'that won't do. Let's fight for our lives, anyhow. Rouse thee, man. Let's work through.'

The other shook his head, but at last rose to his feet, and taking heart of grace from the energy of his companion, who was already at work with his pick, prepared to begin also.

He was stopped by his comrade.

'We can't both dig; we must only make a hole big enough to go through. So while I work you rest, and while you work I'll rest. The boys must take the coal as fast as we break it down, and put it out of our way.'

'But they've no shovels, no baskets, no nothing,' querulously said the listener.

'They've fingers, hands, and jackets. Now for it.'

He began striking as hard, as fast, but also as skilfully as possible, till he was in a profuse sweat, and his strength failing.

Then he stopped, and the other, without a moment's intermission, pursued the work.

And so they went on hour after hour.

The boys meanwhile scraped the coal together with their hands, and ran away with it the moment they had got enough to fill the cavity of their jackets.

No wonder if their fingers soon became raw, but they went on unflinchingly.

And at last, after a lengthened period of dreadful exertion, and still more dreadful suspense and anxiety, they had got through, and were able to reach and stand before Rees Thomas.

A sudden, but faint and distant explosion now spread new alarm through the mass of colliers, and before there was time to speak to them, or arrest their footsteps, as they were running hither and thither, it was followed by another explosion, nearer and far more terrible.

Rees Thomas and a man who had stayed near him, moved by his secret but truly unconscious faith that to be near one so good was almost like a promise of salvation, went to a man-hole near, that happily was big enough to give them partial shelter; and there stooping low as a precaution they heard the burst of an awful thunder-clap, followed by a great hurricane sweeping like a messenger of ruin through the mine.

In an instant they were lifted out like mere playthings for the tempest, and thrown down in the middle of the roadway, both for the moment stupefied.

But Rees Thomas recovered himself almost instantly; and, while his companion lay still sense-less, saw or seemed to see the rolling of the flames—rolling now like the waves of the sea when the lurid light of a burning ship is on them, and now like a snowstorm—to and fro on the varying currents of the wind seeking a way out, and exhibiting (if his eyes did not deceive him through some hallucination of the brain) bright and beau-tiful colours, red, blue, and white; then a moment or two more, and all had passed away; darkness again reigned, and the choke-damp, as the follower of death, came to reap the fruits.

It would seem that the current of air being con-

fined kept the flames in existence unusually long.
And as when they first rushed through the confined
space they kept near the roof, Rees Thomas and
his companion escaped injury then, but on the return of the flames, as they found no instant means
of exit, they came along the bottom, and thus both
the men were sadly burned.

Rees Thomas, in his anxiety about his companion, did not at first know how or where he
was himself injured, beyond the fact of the pain.

A slight wind was felt at that moment, and it
produced such intolerable anguish in Rees Thomas's
face, that his hand went instinctively up to feel ;
and then he knew he was badly burnt; and
his thoughts—for he was human, after all—flying
towards Margaret Doubleday, he felt with the most
exquisite sense of anguish he had yet ever known
that henceforward he would perhaps be intolerable to her very sight.

CHAPTER XI.

DEATH OR VICTORY.

HERE was a new enemy for Rees Thomas to wrestle with, if he would not be utterly overthrown and left helpless, with all these poor wandering men, lost in the deep black darkness, that stretched away from him in various directions; all needing spiritual comfort and guidance, even if he should be unable to render them material help.

He knelt and prayed, and was strengthened.

Margaret became to him once more as a star of light, beckoning to him to arise, deliver these helpless captives, and come forth with them, and have faith in her to glory in her love, rather than to shrink from him because of his misfortune.

Having with his fingers cleared his mouth of the dust which had almost choked him, he put his hand towards his pocket for his tea jack (or can).   Both jacket and tea-can had been blown away.

Again a moment of intense depression ; for even though a man, contending with his own nature, relies upon but little of comfort, he feels keenly the deprivation of that little.

But then again he cried out,

'O my divine Lord and Master, I understand now ! I must lean on, trust to Thee alone, use that Thou hast given me. Thou wilt have me heart and soul in thy service, looking nowhere else for aid and succour. So be it. I am ready.'

And he stood there in that utter darkness, as devoted as was ever the most brave soldier on the most hopeless of missions, ready either for death or victory, calm of heart and clear of brain.

Knowing the importance of excluding the air, he tied a handkerchief carefully over his face, although the touch of the fabric was torture, and then he turned to seek his companion.

After feeling about for some time vainly, he felt the man's shoe, and then gradually feeling along got to his shoulder.

'Sam !' he cried to him.

But there was no answer, except one that was more comforting than painful at that moment—a groan.

'Sam! speak! are you hurt?'

'Ay, ay, I shan't need to fear much more, if that's any comfort!'

The man complained, strange to say, of a bad burn under the arms, though there was no hole in his clothing. In fact he had been in that brief moment of subjection to the tempest so knocked about, that his loose clothing must have been lifted, and hence the burn.

'Oh, Rees Thomas,' he said at last, as opening his over-full heart, 'here's a morning!'

'It is, indeed,' was the reply.

The 'morning' was nearer evening now, but the man had lost all sense of time, and remembered only it had been morning when the calamity opened upon him.

'Rise up, there's a good fellow,' appealed Rees Thomas, for he was lying flat on his breast on the ground, as if he had consciously done with the world, and was seeking the one and only remaining thing, the rest of the grave.

He got up, and his first words were, to the great solace of Rees Thomas,

'Oh, dear Jesus! Let us pray together, let us pray!'

They did both kneel down and pray, the one first thanking God they were still alive, and asking that He would keep them so, if it were His good will, the other supplementing that prayer by one for all the other men who were in the same danger.

The man then wanted to lie down again, but Rees Thomas told him sternly he must come with him.

They took hands, and moved on; the spare hand on each side stretched out to the arm's fullest extent to feel for the sides of the roadway, or for any unexpected obstacles.

Their feet moved nervously at each step, lest they might descend upon the yielding body of a comrade.

They did strike against some form that not long ago had had life, but it proved to be the dead body of a horse.

At that moment a piercing cry went right through Rees Thomas's soul.

It was the voice of a boy crying,

'Mother! Oh, mother! Dear, dear mother!'

'David, is it thee?' rang out the collier-preacher's voice with wonderful power.

For a moment there was no reply, but quickly feet were heard coming, yet as if compelled to pause either from pain and injury, or from the difficulties of the way.

'David, is it thee?'

There was still no answer, save such as was given by the rush upon him of David himself, his heart bursting with anguish, and yet with the sense of possible relief, as he clasped Rees Thomas round the neck, guided to him only by the voice.

After a few moments of joyful embrace, Rees Thomas made a movement to put the lad down; but whether hallucination or fright moved him it was impossible to say, but he clung to him with all the tenacity with which he could possibly cling to life itself; the two indeed seemed confused into the one and same thing.

When Rees Thomas again essayed to put him down, he found the lad's arms and legs immovable, unless he used violence. And at every touch, David began to repeat his cry of 'Oh, mother, mother!' in a voice of such irresistible pathos, that Rees Thomas knew not what to do.

The boy was not heavy, and under ordinary circumstances, and to a man of ordinary strength, the burden might have been of little consequence; here it seemed, even to Rees Thomas, intolerable.

He besought David to stand down for a moment, and he would take him up again in an easier posture, hoping that when he felt he was on firm ground, and was held between the two men, he would grow reasonable; but in the lad's half-madness there was just sufficient method for him to refuse to trust himself away from the shelter of Rees Thomas's breast.

Well, thought the latter, with a sigh, he could but make the attempt. And then he reminded himself that perhaps, after all, this strangely embarrassing incident was the only mode of securing the boy's safety.

So with that weight hanging about him, and

with a cry of pain wrung forth every now and then if he touched David in some particular part— showing he, too, was suffering from burns—the three moved on.

Presently the way was obstructed, and it was some time before they could make out in the darkness what was the obstacle.

It was a mass of trams, huddled together all of a heap, three feet high in one place—a wreck like that on a railway when two trains meet in collision.

Men were lying here, groaning, incapable of removal without fresh aid from without.

Nothing could be more strange or pathetic than the talk, the exclamations, the recognitions in the dreadful darkness.

Rees Thomas was cheered to find no one here dead, and he cheered the wounded men by promising speedy assistance, if only he could get round or through the Fall.

Three roadways met here, and the question was whether to take the main road, leading straight to the Fall, and so to the shaft, or to try one of the two more circuitous and lengthy roads—the ' Nine Feet ' or the ' New vein.'

As the air seemed better, and just breathable, they decided to make straight towards the Fall by the main way.

Sam's failing strength and courage were now utterly exhausted; and on reaching other trams that had been overthrown he doggedly got into one, and refused to answer anything Rees Thomas said to him.

Resting David's form upon the tram while he made his appeal, Rees Thomas got so far relieved that he could go on.

At last the Fall was reached. The first intimation of it was the feet striking against the smaller outlying rubbish near the base.

As he moved on with anxious, uncertain footsteps, the scattered rubbish grew into small heaps, and then into bigger ones, till at last he was stopped; and, kneeling down and stretching out his arms, felt the great slope of protruding beams and masses of rock and coal, ascending out of reach.

'Now, David,' he began; 'listen to me. I am wearied and yet have a great labour to get through. You must help me. We have to make way over this Fall, or find a passage through it, or stay here and die, if no one comes to our help. Which is best?'

The lad relaxed his grasp, and slid to the ground, and there sat in the mournful darkness, but retaining hold of Rees Thomas's clothes.

Hearing his voice, a man called to him, who had also reached the Fall long hours ago, but had found it, he said, too high and too dangerous to go over; for twice he had tried, and in each instance had moved some lightly poised timbers and rock, and narrowly escaped destruction as they came down, heavily falling, past him.

'Have you any tea about you?' asked Rees Thomas, feeling better for the breeze that played all about them, and prepared for new efforts if only he could get something to refresh his burning throat and parched lips.

'Yes. Here it is; take it. Drink it all, if you like, you and the young master'—for Rees Thomas had made known to the man who his companion was.

David drank, and will never as long as he lives forget what that drink was to him. It was balm for his burns, hope substituted for despair, life begun again with all its romance and freshness, just when the boy made sure he was on the threshold of Death!

And then Rees Thomas drank, and returned the jack, still containing plenty of the liquid.

They sat there together a little while in the dense darkness, while Rees Thomas revolved in his own mind, whether in the face of the discouraging report Henry Best had given him, about the danger of trying to ascend the Fall, he had better try, too; or remain patient for a time, to see if succour came from without.

'Has there been anything falling for some time?' he asked.

'No; not since when my feet brought this very timber down we are sitting on.'

'I must try,' said Rees Thomas, earnestly. 'My life is in God's hands. If I succeed, I will soon return to David and to you.'

He rose, but David clung to him, and rose too.

'What now?' asked Rees Thomas, somewhat sternly, though his heart bled for the seeming unkindness.

'I can't stay here. Let me go with you? I must! I will!'

The lad's voice was growing passionate, frenzied. To quiet him, Rees Thomas said,

'You shall if you will listen to me first, and know what you are doing. You heard what Henry Best said?'

'Yes.'

'You know, then, the danger of clambering over this immense and confusing mass of rubbish and beams of timber, with no light to guide us, no earthly power to warn us to step a hair's breadth aside from peril, even if that hair's breadth may be the difference between life and death? You understand that?'

'Yes,' whispered David, below his breath.

'Very well, then. But mind this is no work for cowards, but for men, and boys with the hearts of men. If you do not keep entire control over yourself, you may ruin us both, even while I am opening the path to safety for us both. A sudden gesture of alarm from you may bring down upon us this grim, invisible avalanche of the nether world.'

'I will be quiet and careful! I will, I will, indeed, dear Mr. Rees Thomas!'

'Come then, my youthful hero, and let us see what Providence has in store for us.'

Would Henry Best go, too? He decided one way, and then another, two or three times in as many minutes, but finally refused to move. His burns, he complained, ached so bad, and he was so perished with the cold. If he could but get some brandy!

And now Rees Thomas warned David to stand behind him, on no account to move to either side, to take hold of his coat, and try by feeling with his hands, as Rees Thomas proceeded, to discover where the latter planted his steps, and so as he moved upwards to put his feet on exactly the same places.

'Yes,' said David, nervously.

'Are you ready?'

'Yes,' again responded the boy, taking up his position.

'Now, then, move when I move, stand still as a stone when I stand still.'

'Yes.'

Rees Thomas then moved very slowly round the great masses of the Fall, standing still every yard or two as if listening intently for some sound of wind, or perhaps as if desirous to feel it upon his face, which was exposed on the uninjured side; then going on again.

At last he found what he sought, a direct current of air. This he concluded came over the Fall, unless indeed it should unhappily prove to come through an opening in the pile, which was likely enough to exist, on account of the timbers and props mixed with the débris of rock and coal.·

To make sure he went on till he knew he had examined every part that it was possible for him to reach, and found no other current of air so decided, so hopeful. To that spot he returned, glad to find the same wind mark the same spot, which he knew by a stone he had placed to guide him.

'Now, David, cheery, lad. Think of getting to father and mother—— '

A sob interrupted him.

'Getting to father and mother, and telling them

how you and I led the forlorn hope, and so were able to save all the people left behind. All right?'

' Yes, yes ! '

Rees Thomas then began the perilous ascent.

Feeling first with his hands for one solid step upwards, feeling round it for any moveable source of danger, feeling above it, to learn if all was clear, he at last made the step.

He paused to let David realise what he had done, and he felt the lad's hands were at work in the way he had directed. Then repeating the process he made a second step, and David made his first.

' Excellently done ! ' cried Rees Thomas.

Feeling again, he touched something which moved, fell, and then from above there was a great crash, and a scream from David ; but he did not move, further than to try to shrink into no-thingness, and he called out,

' I am not hurt, Mr. Rees Thomas ! '

' Well done, David ; that was a danger, but it has passed, is exhausted, and so the way is clearer.'

Again a step was made in safety by both,

another, and yet another, when the head of Rees Thomas was met by a decided gust of wind, assuring him he was nearing the top, and seeming to show there was plenty of room to pass over.

And so it proved. Presently both were at the top, half lying on it, while Rees Thomas unconsciously strove to penetrate the absolutely impenetrable darkness in order to see how the greater danger of the descent was to be managed.

He feared broken limbs, life-long injuries, but hardly death, if he considered only the risk of stirring unwieldy masses, and their being precipitated with them to the bottom.

But he knew not but that such a movement might displace some accidental or other support of the roof above, or whatever might be in the roof's place, and so bring down new Falls, burying them in the process.

The first thing was to know whether there was a slope, or a precipitous descent.

He sought about with his hands till he felt a roundish stone. This he set gently rolling, and he heard it knocking against one thing and another, as it rolled down to the bottom and rested.

This was an inexpressible relief to Rees Thomas, who knew well he could not roam about where he was to find a fitting place of descent, as he had done for the ascent.

He turned now and shouted to the man left behind,

'Henry Best! I am on the top and am going down. Will you come?'

The collier came, and guided by their directions, the sound of their voices, and at last by their hands, ascended in safety to where they were.

'Henry Best, stay here till we are down—first because you may endanger us who will be below you, next because you may have the benefit of our experience in going down. We may even find the descent bad for us, and yet leave it good for you.'

'All right,' said Henry Best, who quite appreciated the care displayed for him, and determined not to move, or scarcely even to breathe, till he knew what he was about.

Within a few minutes all were safely landed on the ground, and had the joy of seeing in the distance the faint light of lamps promising speedy help or deliverance.

CHAPTER XII.

A BASE BANQUET.

WHERE was Israel all this time?—Rees Thomas wondered. He and the outside world must have known several hours ago of the calamity, and, it could not be doubted, must have been at work somewhere.

His knowledge of the mine, and of explosions generally, soon made him understand that a long time might have elapsed before any explorers could descend on account of the gas; and then, that they might have found it difficult to work their way to the Fall. And even after accomplishing both these things it might have been thought advisable not to spend precious time in digging through so great a ruin, but to get into the district by another route, so as to render the earliest possible succour to the imprisoned men. And this he subsequently found to be the case.

They had still some distance to go to reach the shaft, and the air was very bad, showing that the regular ventilation, if restored at all, was working as yet but imperfectly.

And as they endeavoured to make way towards that faint and apparently yet far off gleam of lamp-light, the air got worse and respiration more difficult.

They found it better nearer the ground, and so made way as well as they could on hands and knees, in the posture of so many animals, towards the light, which grew clearer, and at last enabled them to see a spectacle that for the moment silenced the party, just as they were about to raise their voices.

There were four men, each with his lighted lamp, sitting on the ground, and four black bottles standing in their midst. One of the men was already drunk, and trying to sing a stave from a popular Welsh air, a drinking song, while a second was trying to hush him, and, finding he could not, solaced himself with another drink from one of the bottles. The other two men looked as if they were not quite easy at their companions' behaviour, or at their own share of the dishonest and base banquet.

Rees Thomas knew them all, and guessed they had been employed to search out for those of the men who might need immediate stimulants. The bottles were, or had been full of brandy, no doubt; a most precious medicine to the miner after the shock of an explosion, from burns, when one of the most trying of secondary effects is the sense of cold. A man while suffering from the intense anguish and heat of his burns in one part of his body, will be shivering miserably through all the rest of his frame.

While Rees Thomas gazed in sadness and resentment upon these men, he saw the drunken one take up one of the bottles to drink, then throw it away with violence, as in disgust to find it empty. Another bottle shared the same fate, and nearly struck David where he cowered shivering, and feeling almost sick to death.

It was the turn of the revellers now to be surprised, as they heard a hollow cry from the direction of the Fall, whence they expected no thing of life to issue.

They stared in alarm. They were ignorant and superstitious; and, going from one extreme to the other, from utter reckless audacity in vice, to slavish fear of consequences, they were almost prepared to expect or believe anything. The drunkard's hand was on the neck of the bottle, and his hair almost stirring with awe and wild terror, as he saw the figure of a man emerge from the darkness, his head wrapped up, and looking so like a ghost, or like some new Lazarus risen from the grave, to confront them in their wickedness, that his feverish blood seemed to suddenly change, and leave nothing but ice in his veins.

Then another figure came also out of the darkness, and then a third.

The banqueters were mute, hardly able to raise a cry, each moment anticipating some dreadful issue, they knew not what.

The forms still advancing, were not recognised till they came close, and then the sight of the men's faces as they knew Rees Thomas and David Mort were before them, would have been a study for an artist.

No guilt could be greater, no shame more

damning than was now revealed in their conscious looks.

Among miners it is one of the very first of laws, as it ought to be one of the first for all men, that of incurring extreme risk, hardship, and severe and unremitting labour to succour their stricken fellows.

These men recollected all this too late, and would have gladly endured much to undo their abominable behaviour.

One of them tried to mutter out an excuse that they had found it impossible to proceed, and that they had been so cold, etc., etc., till Rees Thomas stopped him by the remark,

'Cover your face, man! Cover your faces, all of you, and then try to believe that neither God nor man will see you as you are!'

Disdaining to ask them a question, he examined the remaining bottles, found one full and untouched, the other partly full of brandy.

He made David drink a few drops, also the collier they had brought with them, and then himself drank, the last as usual.

While this was going on, the banqueters had

been taking hurried counsel among themselves, and had asked one of the men least compromised, who had indeed disgraced himself through his weakness in not contending against them, rather than from any desire for the debauch itself, to speak to Rees Thomas in their behalf.

He came close to the latter, very humbly, and in some confusion as to how to discharge his commission, and his task was not rendered more easy by Rees Thomas, who demanded, in a rough voice,

'What do you want?'

'Well, we have made a mess of it, that's clear, and we ain't going to deny but we're a bit ashamed——'

'A bit ashamed!' interrupted Rees Thomas.

'Well, as much as you like o' that. Don't stick us fast to words. But can't we do something yet to redeem our characters? This is a bad job, and will injure us among our fellows. So if you don't want to see us go to the devil——'

'Go! Why aren't you his, soul and body, already, without going? Why they're his choicest morsels, man, those that he doesn't need to fetch.'

'You're uncommon hard upon us, Rees Thomas.

We ain't like you, pious, and good, and all that sort of thing, but we are not devils neither, nor devil's meat, not yet. And I should say that you owe us something, if all you say be true on Sundays.'

'What is that?' asked Rees Thomas, with a perceptible change in his tone.

'Why, when fellows have gone wrong isn't it your place to show 'em the way back, and so help 'em to get right?'

'Come then, Jack Lloyd, I'll test you and these comrades of yours. I have come over the Fall and brought these with me. There are others still on the wrong side, some of them too ill to be moved, without friendly hands and a cordial of some kind. The way is dangerous, but we have passed uninjured. Will you risk it?'

The man held down his head, looked thoughtful and perplexed, and said, 'I'll tell them what you say,' and was going towards the others; but they had heard all, as Rees Thomas indeed had intended they should hear, and called out with hearty vigour they would go.

Foremost now was the drunkard's voice and figure. He had sobered suddenly, and was looking strangely dazed and flushed, but bold and determined.

In brief but cogent words Rees Thomas gave them his experience of the passage, and indicated how they might easily hit the place where he had crossed, since they had lights, while he had none.

'Can you trust yourselves with the brandy?' asked Rees Thomas, glancing doubtfully at the drunkard's haggard and disturbed face, which seemed a sort of chaos of expression.

He spoke then:

'Give the bottles to Jack Lloyd and Osborne. They would have been right enough but for me and my chum here.'

Would it not be better for you to take one yourself?' asked Rees Thomas, as he lifted the lamp that had been given to him, and looked with peculiar significance into the man's eyes.

'What do you mean?' returned the man, flushing in savage defiance; then, as if doubting whether he had not mistaken what had been said, he continued—'Did you ask that, meaning it?'

'Yes.'

'You mean the brandy for the folk there?'

'Yes.'

' You think I might be trusted again with it?'

'Yes.'

' Then as God lives in heaven, I will die to-day
before another drop shall touch my lips; and I
will die, or wash out this foul stain.   Rees Thomas,
I ask you for us all to hold your tongue about
this business till you see the end.   Will you?'

'Will I not! Go, and God be with you.
What do I say? He is with you! be sure of that,
and intending this to be the last day of your old
life, and the first of your new and better one.'

As they were going, he called back one of the
men, he who had been the spokesman of the party,
and whom his quick eye had detected as lacking
the courage, if not the desire of the others, to do
something noticeable to redeem their behaviour.

He then explained how he, David, and the
other man with them, were all three much
burnt and injured, and needed help, and therefore the man called he desired should stay with
them.

The others agreed, and went off, and Rees
Thomas followed them with his eye as long as he

could, as if to judge from their manner of the probabilities of their success.

He heard afterwards that these men saved Lusty, and brought him forth with quite a number of others, who must have perished but for the aid they so heroically rendered; and the upshot was that the three became more talked about in the neighbourhood than Rees Thomas himself, as the burning and shining lights of humanity that had redeemed all the horrors of the mine during this day of alarm.

Fearing still worse injury from the cold that affected them all, and from the wind against the burns, Rees Thomas sent for a bundle of canvas.

Each having been rolled in an entire piece by the aid of their assistant, the late brandy drinker, they went rolling rather than walking on, like so many mummies, towards the shaft; seeing already the faint gleams of the summer evening's light at the bottom.

Here they found Israel hard at work receiving the men, as they came or were brought to him out of the mine; ordering those who were strong and uninjured to help others; carefully attending also

himself to those who were helpless; binding up
wounds temporarily where possible; where it was
not, saying a word that, if it did not exactly seem
one (in sound) of fraternal kindness, certainly
meant well; and all the while despatching as
fast as possible, in the order of their need, the
men from the bottom to the top of the shaft,
having no other means than a bucket; for one
of the explosions had utterly smashed the lifting
apparatus.

Rees Thomas checked David's cry towards his
father which was just about to burst from his
lips, and stayed him with a hand on his shoulder,
while bidding him watch for a few moments his
father's proceedings.

He said no more to David, but left the spectacle
to do its own natural work on the boy's mind.

Israel saw nothing of them till they were so
close behind him that David was able to put out
his hand and touch his father's, just as it was
steadying the bucket for another ascent.

He turned quickly, saw David; turned still
farther round, and saw Rees Thomas; then,
exhibiting no sign of emotion, turned again to the

bucket, and was most careful in helping one of the injured men into it. Then he spoke aloud,

'Another can go with this man.'

'Send David,' said Rees Thomas.

'No, the injured ones first,' was Israel's reply, looking steadily and enquiringly round upon the circle of dark, grimy, earnest faces and yearning white eyes, each longing to be first, yet unwilling to ask.

'He is injured—is burnt,' said Rees Thomas, 'and needs prompt aid.'

'Where?' suddenly demanded the father, looking intently at his boy. 'Not badly, David?

'Father; I can wait.'

Israel looked in his lad's face with such an expression in his own as David had never before seen there.

'You shall, my boy, if it be only that you and I may both think of it hereafter!'

'Mr. Rees Thomas has saved my life, father, and he's very ill.'

'Is he?' Again there was a piercing and most intent look, but this time into the features of the former deputy. 'I can do him good, I think.

Rees Thomas, come; the bucket waits. Lift him in, men. Be very careful.'

Rees Thomas was for a moment inclined to put some one else foremost, but on second thoughts submitted.

Just as the bucket was about to be swung upwards, Israel said aloud, but as if speaking only to the saviour of David's life,

'Rees Thomas, get well, if you please, as soon as possible, for I need a Deputy, and there are people here who think you are right about those morning prayers, so if only discipline be preserved, and work uninterfered with, I am content.'

Waiting no answer, he gave the signal for the ascent.

Rees Thomas closed his eyes with a feeling of being a happy man—a happy, blessed, fortunate man—in spite of the anguish of his burns, and the lassitude that every minute seemed to steal over him, and benumb his faculties.

One single ejaculation alone burst from him, and which was heard by his companion and fellow-sufferer in the bucket with surprise and awe,

'Glory to God! It is His doing!'

CHAPTER XIII.

CASTING BREAD INTO THE WATERS.

On reaching the top, Rees Thomas found a vast crowd of people—men, weeping women, and children—out of whom a certain number had been accepted as assistants. Every one of these was busy tending the wounded, oiling their burns, covering them with wadding, feeding them with food.

A screen of canvas had been hastily put up, with poles, and a piece thrown over as a roof, and there Rees Thomas was taken.

Two or three doctors were at work, but so coolly and deliberately, and so obviously free from the hushed excitement that affects even the medical men most used to the business when the loss of life is serious, that Rees Thomas knew without questioning the general result.

The injuries yet known were few, and as most of the people were already got out of the mine, and the remainder were apparently coming fast to the surface, Dr. Jolliffe felt himself free to comment jocundly on Israel's luck. One man only killed, a few with broken limbs, and that was all as regards the human interests at stake. Then as to the mine itself, why such a calamity, if it must happen, could not possibly have occurred at a more convenient time—when everything was going to be repaired.

To that Rees Thomas put the finishing touch by speaking of David's danger and safety.

By the time Rees Thomas was oiled and bandaged like the rest, and temporarily blinded in the process, he felt so seriously the increasing sense of physical exhaustion, that he almost forgot even to be grateful for the wonderful relief from actual pain that ensued.

Yet even then he could not but ponder over the look of concern he had seen settle on Dr. Jolliffe's face when he first took off the wrappings, and saw the nature of the injury to the right cheek.

Permanent disfigurement—ah, yes! That was what the doctor saw, he thought, and what Margaret Doubleday would see ere long.

His fortitude seemed at that moment really giving way. It was not one thing, but many things that gathered like shadows of evil and misfortune about him, each affecting him with its own peculiar and depressing influence, till the whole became overwhelming.

As he was preparing to be led home by a brother collier, news came that some friend in the village, a farmer, having heard of his accident, had brought a little chaise to carry him.

To that he was conducted by kind hands, and there found everything, even in so short a time, had been most tenderly studied for his warmth, and ease, and comfort. There were cushions to support his weak frame, wrappers for warmth, beef tea in a bottle for immediate sustenance.

His heart was touched, and his soul was full of remorse to God, for his late graceless doubts and repinings.

After secretly disburdening himself in prayer

and praise, he could not but turn full of emotion
to his friend who was driving the pony with
unusual carefulness, in order to keep an even pace
and smooth motion.

'Why did you take all this trouble for me?' he
asked, reproachfully.

'Could I do less for one who has saved my
life?' was the answer, and the low peculiar tone
surprised the hearer as much as the words.

'Your life? What can you mean, Morris?'

'Do you not know?'

'No, indeed!'

'Nor suspect?'

'Indeed, and indeed, no!'

'Well, before I knew you, I was getting into
that bad way, that at last I thought there could
be no extrication. I tried to read the Bible you
had given me, and which I jested over when you
gave it. The more I read, the darker everything
seemed to grow, till I couldn't bear to open it.
One day when I was passing the pool near the
limekiln, I threw it in, that I mightn't be tempted
to try any more.

'As I watched with a sort of devilish satisfaction

the Bible sink, I found a strange jumble of things in my brain, jostling one another. I wanted to see if I should sink and be as easily done with as the book. And then I wanted to fetch the book out again. And yet how was I to manage that without coming out myself, too?—which I was clean against, if once I got in.

'Just then, by some strange chance, as I thought it, you came by and spoke to me. I saw you had no suspicion of me, and I was glad. I don't know what you said, and I can't remember anything I said, but there was something in your look, your voice, and your whole manner that made me think, while my hair stood up on my head the while, that you were supernaturally sent to me, not even yourself knowing of your mission.

'When you left me, I found a sheltered corner, and there knelt and prayed.

'Then I leapt into the water, and tried vainly to find my Bible.

'It had sunk into the soft muddy bottom.

'I seemed to think it *must* be got out; that my whole future salvation depended on getting it out. Again, and again, and again I tried, till my strength was all gone. My teeth were chattering with cold, and I stood there shivering, like a lost soul, in the bleak wind. Well, I would die or get it out, I thought once more. So after revolving the matter a bit as to the precise spot, which I might have mistaken, I ventured farther in, there found it, and brought it forth. No man could feel what I felt then, and not love the book ever after. It is *here* now, Rees Thomas, near my heart.'

Then controlling his voice, and speaking more calmly, he added, after a pause,

'So you won't wonder any more, I hope, if I try, so far as my little means go, to show you what I think and feel.'

Rees Thomas had no time to reply, much as he desired, for they were now but a few yards from the door of his house.

He wondered, perhaps felt hurt, that he had seen nothing of Margaret among all the other tearful and anxious women at the pit's mouth.

Mrs. Mort he had seen there, conspicuous in the crowd, wringing her hands like a wild creature, and crying out,

'Where is he? My boy David! Why do they not bring him up?'

He would gladly have spoken to her, but could not conveniently, and so his eyes had passed away in their search for Margaret.

Not finding her he had hoped that she and her mother had happily remained ignorant of all.

He wished, therefore, now to be the first to tell her.

With the aid of Morris—the kind farmer—he walked to the little gate, and through the little bit of front garden, still hearing for a moment or two no sound.

Then he heard the door open hurriedly, and stretching out his hand as if he were indeed a blind man, called out:

'Margaret!'

'Rees Thomas! Hurt! Oh, mother, mother! Come! Come! Quick!'

'Thou hast but to thank God with me, Margaret, for His mercies and for His chastisement. Be not afraid. All will be well!'

So saying, he shook his friend by the hand, said a few words, and hurriedly wished him good-bye.

Then he felt for Margaret's hand, and guided by this—all trembling as he felt it was—passed over the threshold, and shut the door after him, which was not again to be opened for him to go forth to work for many a day.

CHAPTER XIV.

NEW HOPES AND FEARS.

EVER thoughtful of others, and feeling a special interest in and love for the boy, Rees Thomas's last words to the farmer had been to ask him to go back again to the mine, and do for David and his mother what he had done for him.

Morris found the boy just out of the doctor's hands; who pooh-poohed the idea of anything serious, said he would be all right again in a few days, and tried to make David laugh by saying to him he had been only winning his spurs after the old knightly idea, a little modernised in the mode of appliance.

David grew cheerful and animated on the way home. He highly appreciated the conveyance, and the cushions that protected his weary frame and his burned shoulder, and he luxuriated in the sense of the great relief from pain he enjoyed.

But these things, after all, did not make up the whole or even the most essential part of David's change of feeling. Something much more sweet was acting on his wounded spirit as a precious balm. He had not, after all, been such a coward.

Or, if he had, people didn't know it, and they did know what he had said to his father.

Already he had heard his father's men talking of it, and looking at him, while he was waiting for the doctor to dress his wound; and he had not quite known whether he ought to be ashamed or proud—ashamed they should think so much better of him than, on the whole, he deserved—proud that they were not mistaken, at all events, in the matter they talked of.

What a story he had to tell his mother on the way home! Othello's to Desdemona was nothing to it. Nor was the lady's receptive belief in all the dangers and wonders told to her, to be compared, for a moment, with Mrs. Mort's acceptation of David's narrative. And as Rees Thomas played in it so significant a part, the listener who drove them was scarcely less interested. And he thought how he would like to tell Rees Thomas on his bed of sickness some of these things if he could only recollect the words.

Some days have passed, and have brought a change over David. He is nearly well in body; but, as he improves in that respect, he suffers proportionally in mind. Each day, each night, each meal, reminds him how soon the work in the mine must begin again. And ever the thought of it grows more and more one of utter disgust.

He fights against this insidious enemy bravely. He believes what his mother says, that it is disuse has brought back the old horror of the mine, and that use will drive it away. He owns that his father may be right in saying he will benefit through his whole life afterwards by the knowledge and practical familiarity and general discipline that will grow out of such squalid and humiliating labour. In fact, he objects to nothing but her conclusion,—

' My dear boy, you must go back to the mine.'

He says nothing even to that, remembering how often and with what passionate antagonism he had responded to such sayings ; but not the less does he feel he would give all he has in the world—and as that is not very much, why, then, a good deal of all he ever hopes to obtain—to be allowed to go to some other occupation. He does not care what, if only his father would consent, and find one for him. There is hardly any trade, employment, or form of industry that does not grow positively winning in its attractiveness when looked at beside the mine, with its foulness and ever-attendant dangers, its grave-like depths, and ghostly suggestiveness.

He knows all the same he must do it. And the knowledge gives new intensity and strength to his hatred of the work. His mind is growing, its powers enlarging ; he begins partly to perceive and understand this, but also feels increasing bitterness with his fate, becomes more inclined to be rebellious, if only he knew how to resist, and what else to do.

Dimly, vaguely, the thought steals in upon him now and then, Can he not run away, and earn his livelihood in his own manner, how and where he pleases? Why not? Other boys have done this and succeeded, and have become great men. Why not he?'

But when he begins in thought to realise the idea, to trace his course among strangers, to whom he could be no other than poor boys were about his own neighbourhood to the people who lived there, some of whom he had seen in rags, and picking out of dust heaps by the street side morsels of carrot, lumps of stale bread, parings of apples and potatoes—when in his ignorance of the world at large he tried to understand it, and was driven for means of comparison to his own limited experience, he shrank back in affright, and found even the mine a shelter, and his father a friend.

The last day of his convalescent leisure has arrived. Once more he is combating with his difficulties, and finds one peculiar mode of help without being willing to acknowledge it. Being as he is, ever in fear of seeing the word coward flaming before him and before the eyes of the world, he is in constant alarm that some moment of trial, of call, will come to him, and he will fail to answer it.

This ever-present fear often drives him consciously to subject himself to manly and robust
influences, that otherwise his temperament would
instinctively have shrunk from.   It influences
him now to come at last to the conclusion to say
to his father he is ready, without waiting for the
latter to summon him.

Thinking that well over, it pleased him, and
in pleasing it strengthened him.   And so his
cheerfulness began to return.

In the evening when Israel came home (the
accident already sufficiently cared for, and forgotten), his hands and pockets full of papers—
plans, accounts, estimates, etc.—David was able
not only to say the thing he had resolved on,
but so to say it that Israel was even more im-
pressed with the manner than with the matter—
a most uncommon result.

He looked at the lad's pale but still bright face
steadily.   The blue frank eyes looked back with
no sign of shrinking or furtiveness, and then Israel
held out his hand, grasped David's little one
warmly, and said,

'I shall be proud of thee yet, lad!' and went

away without another word, as if the matter were done with for some years to come.

A recollection of something brought him back.

'What's that the doctor says about the burns being where some injury had happened before? He looked at me, as if he thought I had given you some cruel flogging. Did I?'

'No, father!' responded David, passing his hand over his face, to conceal how it had suddenly flushed to the hue of scarlet.

'Well?' said Israel impatiently, after a pause, and wondering what the boy's change of colour and his behaviour might mean.

David in those few moments was in an agony of doubt and irresolution. Should he lie? And then what lie would do to satisfy a man like his father? Coward! That word again confronted him. The truth should out. The affair was so long ago that no harm could happen if he did tell.

Such were the thoughts that swept in rapid sequence through David's brain in those few seconds of time that passed while Israel waited for his answer. And then in broken, almost incoherent language, he told the story of the horsewhipping.

Then for the first time in his life did David see how his father could be moved.

The stony insensibility of his features changed into a fixed expression that was fearful. His lips visibly whitened with rage.

He walked slowly away in dead silence, and stood by the window looking out.

Then, as if that did not suit him, he turned, and his face being away from David, looked down on the ground, as if there only, in the wit and sagacity of mother Earth, was to be found the counsel he sought.

He came back, and made David tell the story a second time, which he did much more intelligibly; as Israel had got enough out of the first narrative to guide him in the method.

Then he called in his wife; who, busy in the kitchen preparing some little delicacy for David which Israel was not to know of, remained ignorant of the discovery.

Seeing the look on his face, she dropped in her fright the floury knife she had held in her hand,

and stood as one appalled, conscious of a coming and fearful revelation, yet unable even to guess at its nature.

'Did you know of this—?'—he paused as if unwilling to use the right word, yet too proud to disguise the matter of it by weaker ones, 'this—horsewhipping—of David?'

Whether David feared his mother's weakness, the usual vice by which the victim tries to evade the harshness of the oppressor, and saw it could only make matters worse, as discovery was certain; or whether it was simply the desire to speak for her, as she seemed unable to speak for herself, he at all events called out hurriedly,

'Father, I didn't intend to tell anybody, because'—he paused a little as if confused; 'because I was so ashamed, and because,'—there he paused again.

'Because?' repeated Israel, in his most dangerous tone and mood,—

'Because I thought it better to bear it in silence, than make mischief; but I wasn't man enough to keep it from mother, and—and I was obliged to have something done to—'

'Take off his bandages!' cried Israel harshly, interrupting the boy.

They were taken off, and Israel was able to see the marks still remaining of the severe cuts received from Mr. Griffith Williams's whip.

'Ah, that will do! Wrap him up again. I was afraid there might be no sufficient signs left. How long is it since?'

David told him, and Israel reckoned up the days, and looked almost vindictively at his wife, that she should, by keeping him in ignorance, have left it almost a matter of doubt whether he could obtain what he intended if possible to exact—aye, even if necessary at the price of all he owned in the world—redress.

But the thought of the greater criminal, and of all that might be necessary to bring him to justice, weakened the temptation to trouble about the lesser one, so for a wonder she escaped; but in doing so was conscious she would have to be on her best behaviour, and not dare to intervene in any way, by word or act, between him and Griffith Williams's punishment.

He went upstairs to the bed room, and they

could hear his footsteps going towards a closet, where he kept many private things he valued.

David and his mother looked at one another with increasing alarm, but said nothing, and listened intently.

Not a sound could they hear, and that fact struck them as unusual, portentous, as if Israel were meditating something so serious, that even he went out of his way to study how best to keep his movements and gestures unknown to those below.

Nothing more alarming than that fact, if it were true, could well happen to the two listeners.

At last they heard him moving again freely as before, and then he came down, and went out and left them.

Sad and full of misgivings were the hearts of those who remained, knowing nothing of his intentions—whether he would retaliate in kind, or publicly expose the offender, or go to law, as before, and get heavy damages, or resort to even worse measures.

'Oh mother, mother!' cried David, after an ineffectual attempt to restrain his tongue. 'If he has been to fetch his revolver, the one Mr. Jehoshaphat gave him when he used to go to the Bank! Do go up and see!'

Mrs. Mort went, found the cupboard locked, but remembered it had been only accidentally left open. No conclusion either way, therefore, could be drawn. And this satisfied Mrs. Mort for the time. But not so David, who again cried out,

'Oh mother, he is going to the Farm; he will kill her father!'

CHAPTER XV.

ISRAEL'S EVENING RIDE.

ABOUT this time Israel did a thing that excited no little comment among his neighbours, and afforded them no little amusement. He appeared one day on the road from Leath, after the annual cattle-market, mounted on a powerful and reasonably good-looking brown mare.

When any acquaintance met or passed him, and smiled, nodded, or made some remark about his new purchase, he answered the nod, smile, or remark with imperturbable good humour; and went his way, aware that everyone stopped and looked after him, to study such an unwonted spectacle. But he did not get nervous therefore, or appear restlessly shifting his seat, or stiffening himself to sit more upright, or seeming to be so much at ease that he could afford to busy himself in the study of the landscape, like other equestrian novices on their first essay, when exposed to criticism.

Whether he had taken lessons on some of his necessarily frequent visits of business to Leath, no one knew; but after the first general laugh at the oddity of his appearance, it was decided by common consent he would ride well enough in time, because he was so lithe, and so fearless.

And then too it began to be discovered, with that wisdom after the event that so happily characterises the world of gossipers, that a horse must be very useful to Israel in his new position, and they only wondered he hadn't thought of so sensible a thing before.

Had they known why Israel chose that precise period of time to begin to ride, their interest in his movements would have been marvellously quickened just when they began to slacken in their observation. An incident revealed the truth about the horsemanship to at least one person, Mr. Griffith Williams.

Just a week had elapsed from the time of Israel's discovery of how his boy had been treated by the Squire, and it was beginning to be supposed at home that he had forgiven, or forgotten the offence in his many absorbing occupations.

It was market-day at Leath, and drawing towards evening—a cool, delicious summer's evening—just such a one as might be supposed to tune men's hearts to peace and accord, and leave it impossible for feuds or strifes of any kind to exist for the time being. At this hour, when earth and sky seemed to vie with each other in serene tender beauty, when the sun had just gone down, but left much of his splendour behind him, and the moon was just rising faint, but inexpressibly sweet, and seeming to call forth one by one the lovely and interminable procession of stars around her, it was then that Israel appeared just under the shadow of some lofty trees, sitting his brown mare like a statue, with uplifted hand holding his heavy riding whip at the lash end, the handle resting on his knee.

Strange to say, he had not, like most other horsemen on the road, come from market, on his way home. He had come from his home to this spot, there taken his stand, and waited.

To those who came from Leath, he was entirely hidden till they turned the corner, and then they met him face to face. Anyone else, knowing his own purposes, would have found it difficult to meet so many eyes questioning him, and have moved about from time to time, to conceal the fact he wanted to be stationary. But Israel apparently was content to know that if he attained his object, these people's thoughts wouldn't trouble him, and that he was most likely to attain his object by staying where he was.

But he started into sudden activity when a horseman approached, going towards Leath. He advanced to meet him, shook hands, became curious, for a wonder, as to where his acquaintance was going, but relapsed into his own thoughts, and went back to his place of shelter, the moment he found the horseman was not going more than a few yards before he would turn off towards his own farm.

' He knows us both, and would be sure, if they had met, to say he had seen me, and here,' Israel commented to himself as he again glanced through the tall brushwood against which he stood, and looked along the road.

He had thus waited, perhaps nearly three quarters of an hour, when he heard a loud cheery voice calling out, and others farther off answering it.

'Ah! All right!' he thought, as he felt and shook the reins, took his whip by the handle, and, leaning just a little forward, listened intently, and once more motionless.

He could hear by the things they said, by their jovial laughs that any trifle sufficed to call forth, and by the tone of their voices, they were all somewhat elated by liquor, and coming along in a very irregular fashion—cantering, trotting, walking, all within a very short distance.

' They must stop, anyhow, to pass round the corner,' Israel said to himself, as he gently moved his horse a pace or two forwards—in fact as far as he could go without being seen.

' Well, good night, gentlemen!' called out a voice exceedingly near—and that the voice of Mr. Griffith Williams. 'I shall leave you and gallop off home!'

'Good night!'—'Good night!' replied some half-dozen voices in chorus, and Griffith put spurs to his horse, and dashed into the partial shade made by the angle of the road and the over-arching trees.

But almost as suddenly as he started did he stop, throwing his horse on to his haunches by the violence he used, for he saw a horseman advance from the brushwood on the right, almost as if he leaped into the road, turn, and face him —so exactly in the line of his own movement as to show he meant mischief.

A second glance showed who the horseman was, and then Griffith understood what was the true meaning of Israel's new accomplishment—it was simply to facilitate getting at him, who was almost always on horseback, riding about the country for sport or exercise, or for the agreeable duties of his farm.

The laugh that was his first impulse died out when he saw the look and attitude of Israel, and he remembered, almost like a thing that had happened long ago, how he had treated David.

He had no fear of Israel—except as regards

the thoughts of the public, should any fresh scandal arise from this evidently intended meeting.

He glanced back, before either had spoken, and saw his companions just at his heels, and thought it would certainly be well, if possible, to avoid the disgrace of a vulgar personal contest. He remembered too his own later thoughts about the propriety of his dealing with David, and so felt altogether a real and earnest desire to let no more evil happen at present—and on that lovely night—and while he was yet in all the jovial good fellowship of spirit excited by wine and the society of his companions.

Thus he was for the moment silent and still, though his mettlesome steed struck the ground repeatedly, as if to ask If his master wanted to gallop, why didn't he?

Israel's steed, on the contrary, was like its master—silent, motionless, grim.

The other gentlemen, mostly persons of Griffith's own rank, or large tenant-farmers, now noticed the two men thus facing each other in so still and remarkable a manner, and instantly the cry went round—' Israel Mort!' 'What does the fellow want?' 'Let's ride him down!'

Griffith's upraised arm stopped the execution of this feat—if indeed it were anything more than a bubble of reckless friendship just blown out of the fumes of the wine they had been drinking, and which would have at once evaporated in attempting to be practical.

'Two words to that, before you try,' said the hard voice of Israel. 'I have no quarrel with you, nor you with me. Go your way. This gentleman and I have a little private business to do together, which I think he would prefer being done in private.'

Seeing, however, their only reply was a general laugh, and then a hurried discussion among themselves, he addressed himself to Griffith.

'It was not a very manly thing, Mr. Griffith Williams, to horsewhip my boy—to lash him so that even yet the marks are to be seen; but I do you the credit to believe you are, in spite of that ugly fact, not quite so mean or cowardly as to shelter yourself behind all these respectable gentlemen, to whom I say once more—Pass on, and leave us alone to the settlement of our account.'

Then in a louder, sterner, and almost excited tone, he said—'You see, do you not? I don't attack him as he attacked my boy, by surprise. I leave that to squires and gentlemen. No, I come here armed with my wrong, and this riding whip. He has the same kind of weapon, and I here offer to exchange with him if he thinks I have played any foul tricks with mine. But go from here he does not, nor do I, till I have larned him something or he has larned it to me!'

'And suppose,' said Griffith, whose choler was fast rising, 'I don't choose to degrade myself in such a fashion?'

'Then I choose to do the job for you.'

'On, gentlemen! Out of the way, rascal!' shouted Griffith, spurring his horse, intending by the sudden onset to overthrow Israel, if the latter did not move; but he, also spurring his mare, a more powerful animal than the blood chestnut ridden by his antagonist, drove sideways against the other—and shook the animal and its rider so violently, that for the moment it was all Griffith could

do to retain his seat; and that moment Israel used
to strike him—so fiercely, that he felt his face and
brow were cut ; the blood gushed forth, blinded
him, and before he knew well what he was doing
or should do, he had fallen heavily to the ground,
and was rolling in the dust of the summer road,
while his horse madly galloped away, and was
lost even to the sight of the gentlemen who
witnessed the scene.

Before they had time to decide what they had
best do, Israel had slid from his mare, and at the
very moment that Griffith, stupefied, had risen a
little on to his hands and knees, Israel was over
him, and lashing him with the strength of an arm
that made every blow a severe injury, an intolerable torture.

He had struck thus perhaps half-a-dozen times
when he found himself surrounded by the other
gentlemen, and his motions impeded, while one
hand even clasped his wrist.

He became at once collected, calm, and said
almost with a smile,

' Don't be alarmed, gentlemen, enough's as good
as a feast. I have done. I ask you all to report

the facts as they happened, just as they happened!'

He looked at every one of the scowling, angry faces, which showed the owners would like to horsewhip him in return, or arrest him as a malefactor; but as he passed through them, recommending them to see to their friend, they did nothing, and he went to his brown mare, got up, and rode off, never once looking behind.

CHAPTER XVI.

SUMMONS *v.* SUMMONS.

WHAT would any man of moderately good sense and average power of judgment have done, in Griffith Williams's position, supposing such qualities and position to be at all compatible? Surely, he would have eaten his leek, or as Lusty phrased it, when expressing his opinions about the matter, have grinned and bore, knowing that he had given the provocation, and that the more the affair was talked of, the worse it must be for him.

Of course, therefore, that was just what Mr. Williams did not do. By the side of this outrage upon him, his own on David seemed to become too trivial to engage the attention of sensible men. His friends were to a man ready to testify that he had done nothing at the meeting to justify Israel's ferocious attack. He was a magistrate, and felt convinced that his brother magistrates would resent such an atrocity done on a member of their order. Finally he had no longer the restraint that fear of publicity had before given. Everybody knew of the circumstance; the local papers were full of it, and when in sheer disgust of reading even friendly notices in them, he turned to his London daily, the very first thing that attracted his eye was a paragraph headed, A MAGISTRATE HORSEWHIPPED.

Before he went home that night he had obtained, not what he wanted, a warrant for the arrest of Israel Mort, but a summons for the next meeting of the Petty Sessions.

This was executed immediately, the man employed forcing his way into Israel's bed chamber to serve the summons, and serving it upon him in bed.

The alarm and distress of Mrs. Mort and David may be easily imagined, as they, both trembling, and fancying that perhaps some great crime had been committed to obtain their late prosperity, followed the man up the stairs, David in his night

shirt, having been waked by the clamour of the
man outside wanting to see Mr. Mort par-
ticularly.

Israel sat up, took the document in one hand,
and a candle in the other, and read it through,
then said to the man,

'Very well. You'll have one to serve for me
in the morning. Good night.' He then adjusted
his night-cap, turned, and addressed himself again
to sleep.

His wife and son, having followed the
stranger downstairs, and fastened the door after
him, sat down, and gazed blankly on each other's
faces.

'It's all coming out now, mother!' said David,
in a tone of the deepest, most passionate despair.
'I thought it would! Father's going to get a summons against Mr. Williams for beating me! I
shall have to be in court—and—and—Nest will
hate me all her life if her father gets punished and
disgraced, and all through me. And if she
doesn't, it'll be all the same. She'll never be able
to speak to me! And she'll get older, and feel
she's rich, and beautiful, and that I was but a

collier's boy, and that her father had whipped me like one of his dogs—and—but mother, I won't go! No, that I will not!'

'Won't go where, David?'

'Not to the court, to speak against Mr. Griffith. I couldn't. No—not if father were to use me worse than Mr. Griffith, or to bribe me by saying I should go no more down into the mine.'

'Hush, David—hush! Or the father will hear.'

She drew him nearer to her, made him nestle in her loving bosom, and there they sat, and talked over plans that had been for some time seething in the brain of David, and which now for the first time he found his unhappy mother willing to listen to.

And in talking, in low, earnest, pathetic tones, they forgot how time was passing; and when at last David lay down in his little cot, and his mother kissed him, he had to ask her to draw down the blind, for already it was daybreak.

Israel, on his part, was also wakeful. Not disturbed in the least by the summons, or by the new contest he must engage in, of summons against summons, counter-charge against charge; no, he with clear eye saw that the issue could be of no serious moment to him, even if he got the worst, and dismissed it, characteristically, till the morrow, when there would be something to do.

No, he was not thinking of Mr. Griffith Williams, and the summons against him to be taken out, or of the crowded court that would soon have to be faced, or even of what his wife and son might be now thinking or suffering through the summons.

And yet he was thinking at last of David, as David had so long hopelessly yearned for him to think. He was conning over a number of little incidents of the boy's behaviour in the mine, and of some rather striking words dropped almost accidentally by Rees Thomas about the lad's bright future; and he was seriously weighing the question how much longer it might be necessary, for the sake of the discipline and practical know-ledge involved, that David should work in the pit.

He could not, or would not decide that question now, but he thought the boy deserved some encouragement, and he would see if it could be given without upsetting him.

It so happened, however, that he said nothing till the morning when they had all to go to Leath, for the hearing of the case.

They breakfasted very early ; and Israel, remembering what he had resolved to do, his thoughts naturally busied themselves more than ordinarily on the subject of David. Thus he came to take more notice than was usual with him, and so became aware, as he supposed, how deeply both wife and son were affected by the business of the day.

Not choosing to consult with them on such a subject, or indeed to speak of the affair at all— looking upon David's part in it as such a mere matter of course that it was not even worth while questioning him about it in advance—he still, with a feeling unusual with him, set himself to ease the hearts of both, if he could, on much more important matters.

' Wife,' said he, ' you will be glad to hear that David gets on so fairly that there'll be no need for him to stay long down below.'

'Indeed!' said Mrs. Mort, with an air that was
more like that of pained surprise, than of the
sudden burst of joyful gratitude Israel expected.
And then her eye seemed wistfully to seek
David's, who determinedly looked down.

'Indeed!' said he, sternly repeating her word.
'Doesn't that suit thee—or David?'

'Oh yes, indeed!'

'Then don't interrupt. You break the chain of
my thought, and it takes time and patience to
get it straight again. Where was I? Aye, David,
thou shall see, in a few months most likely, what
it is I have been working for. I shall send thee to
a college I know of, where thou will get an
education fit for a prince; and larn all the sciences
that bear upon mining business; and then, after a
spell of that, you shall go under a good man I
know, who has the management of a whole lot of
mines, so that you can get among 'em every sort of
experience; and then thou shall come back and be
my agent a year or two, and then come out at last
as a whole company, in thy single self, for Israel
Mort and Co. will be just us two. What does
thou say to that, David—and thou too, wife?'

Both were much moved, and deeply grateful, and so far Israel's experiment had been a successful one. But if he had been more accustomed to read the faces of those about him, and who should have been dear to him—nay, who were dear to him in a sort of fashion—he would have seen something in the manner of both, heard something in the tones of both, of warning, and of the necessity that he should at once probe the matter to the bottom.

But he was too much engrossed by his worldly cares to see more than they desired he should see, and perfectly content that they accepted his scheme as one of no ordinary value.

It had been arranged that they were to be ready at eight o'clock, dressed in their best clothes; when Israel would send a light cart, and careful driver, to take both to the court-house at Leath.

But David, as the time came for his father to go forth, could not help, it seemed, in the gratitude of his heart, coming close to Israel's chair, and taking his hand, and kissing it; and dropping on his knees on a little stool that stood there; and at last clasping his father round the waist, and bursting out into a passion of tears, and sobs, and broken speech.

All Israel could get out of the boy's words was David's sorrow for so misunderstanding him, and giving him so much trouble; and his yearning desire to be forgiven and to be thought as well of as possible in the future.

And then, just as David's gratitude became almost oppressive, Mrs. Mort must join in, and Israel had to pass his arm round her, and quiet her excitement, inexplicable as it seemed to him. But he was in the mood either to feel he could respond to the affection exhibited, or seem to do so, very happily.

Shall we attempt to look into the innermost recesses of Israel's heart as he saw himself once more master of the hearts of those two persons? Shall we ask whether he consciously played the hypocrite, a character certainly not natural to him, while seeming to recur to old days when the affections did occupy some part—however small —of his moral framework, and when he had not yet put on, with almost ostentatious cynicism, the air of a man who acknowledges no brotherhood with his kind? Shall we ask such questions? Let us first be sure we can to a certainty justly answer them. Good and evil are so inextricably mingled in human motive that often when even character itself seems to tell us trumpet-tongued by its actions, what must have been the impelling power to this good or to that evil, we have often but to live on a few years more to find we were utterly mistaken and unjust.

For the present, then, at least, let us suspend judgment, and be content to wait and watch.

CHAPTER XVII.

ON THE BENCH.

THE court-house was crowded. There was a full bench of magistrates, and every spare seat on the bench was occupied by noblemen and gentlemen resident in the neighbourhood; who had heard of this, the latest incident of the war between Israel Mort and his former employer; and wanted to see the leaders of the fray, and watch the fortunes of the legal fight.

Mr. Griffith Williams had engaged counsel, but Israel absolutely forbad his lawyers to copy his example. He would conduct his own case, and all he asked was, they should instruct and guide him as to forms.

Some minor cases had to be gone through first, and then there was full opportunity for the spectators to study the aspect, persons, and behaviour of each of the now renowned combatants.

Griffith was on the bench, a part of his face
and brow and one eye covered with black silk,
to conceal the wound and its dressings. Israel
was in the body of the court where the lawyers
sat.

The first thing that startled the ears of the
auditory was Israel's harsh demand, the moment
the case was called on, that Mr. Griffith Williams
should do what he—Israel—was obliged to do,
occupy a place in the body of the court.

'It seems to me, Sir,' he said, ' that as a magistrate among magistrates, Mr. Griffith Williams
cannot possibly be also a defendant, standing
before the court for judgment in a case where he
is charged with wanton cruelty to a boy of tender
years.'

There was some murmuring and putting of
heads together on the bench at this appeal, and
Mr. Griffith Williams rose, and in a gentlemanly
way that could not altogether conceal that he
trembled with excitement or repressed passion at
Israel's audacity, offered at once to resign his
privilege, and descend to the place suggested.

Here the chairman interposed, and said in bland

accents, after a shrewd glance round, that told him there was no vacant seat—

'It is no question of privilege, Mr. Mort, but of convenience. You see how crowded the court is. You are quite welcome to find a place here too, if you can.'

'Thank you, Sir,' said Israel, 'that is sufficient. Personally I don't care a straw about the matter.' And so saying, he showed by his quiescent attitude, he did not intend to try his chances for a place on the bench.

The summons first issued was first about to be inquired into, when Israel again raised his voice, and remembering the hint given by his lawyers, who were shocked by the 'Sir,' he said—

'Your worship will, I am sure, permit me to say that the two assaults charged are in effect one affair; and therefore, to get at the bottom of it, it is necessary you should first hear my charge against Mr. Williams, as that alone can explain his having the opportunity to bring a charge against me.'

Then fancying from their behaviour and what few words he could catch, that they were about to

ignore his demand, he said in a loud voice, that
rang through the court :—

'He horsewhipped my boy, and I horsewhipped
him ; therefore you'll be putting the cart before
the horse if you begin with his charge, and not
with mine !'

Again Mr. Williams, as if determined to support
with dignity an undignified position, interposed;
and added his wish that Mr. Mort's charge
should be first gone into, and for doing which his
lawyer whispered he might lose the cause.

'Where is the boy?' asked the chairman, thus
putting a question to Israel that Israel had put to
himself many times during the last few minutes,
and with increasing anger every time.

'I am expecting him, every minute,' replied
Israel. 'I fear some accident has happened to the
vehicle.'

There was at this period some little confusion and
noise at one of the smaller doorways leading into
and out of the court, which at first was supposed
to be merely the effect of the pressure ; but it
soon appeared that a man, with his hat elevated to
keep it out of harm's way, was struggling to pass

through the dense mass of the people, and reach the place where Israel was.

At last he managed to catch Israel's eye, and was at once recognised as the driver who had been sent to fetch Mrs. Mort and David.

With some effort, aided by the officers of the court, Israel got to him; and heard with blank astonishment that the driver found no one in the house, and that after waiting some minutes he judged they must have gone by some other conveyance.

' Were you after your time?' demanded Israel harshly.

' No, rather before it,' replied the man, ' as the neighbours will tell you.'

' The neighbours, had they seen them go? Did you ask?'

' Yes, but no one had seen them.'

Israel knew at once his cause was lost. He was before hostile judges. His wife and son were alike absent, and were the only parties who could have proved the character and amount of the original injury.

Suddenly he remembered the doctor ; and called out in a loud voice,

" Is Dr. Jolliffe here ? " There was no response. Israel's case was hopeless.

Still he hesitated not a moment to demand a postponement of the inquiry, and was very curtly interrupted by Mr. Griffith Williams's counsel, who treated the demand as absurd, and appealed to the Court to proceed with their charge—the only real one, no doubt, though Mr. Mort had tried to hoodwink them, while getting up some trivial or imaginary case.

The chairman decided promptly to go on, and leave it to Israel to proceed at some future day if he pleased with his own complaint as an independent case.

The counsel called witness after witness who had been present at the encounter on the previous evening, and their evidence was clear against Israel that he had been lying in wait, that he had compelled Mr. Griffith Williams, in self-defence, to the only hostile act committed by the latter—the spurring his horse with the intention of forcing his way past, and that he had then been struck most

savagely, knocked off his horse, and again lashed
severely before they could get to him, and inter-
pose.

Israel looked at each witness in succession, as if
he had the power of searching their very hearts, but
declined to cross-examine, or ask any questions.

The evidence against him being ended, he was
asked what he had to say.

'Nothing,' he replied, ' but this: I have told
you before, and I tell you again, he treated my
boy most cruelly—and this I could have proved
if you had thought proper to wait!' Then as if
for a moment stung into entire abandonment of
all that ordinarily strong self-control that he was
master of, he dashed his heavy fist down upon the
table before him, and his voice rang clear and
loud through the court, as he exclaimed, ' And I
will prove it yet—but not before you, unjust
judges that you are! *There* is the true criminal,
sitting among you—one of yourselves—and I was
a fool to come here, and expect to be righted.
End the farce if you please, and let me go!'

This was not a very prudent speech to make,
and it naturally made every magistrate on the

bench, biassed perhaps before, decidedly hostile now ; and inclined to punish him severely, that is to say, with imprisonment for a longer or shorter period.

But there was something in the man's earnest conviction and indomitable fearlessness, that suggested there might be truth in his allegation about the boy ; and that if so, it behoved the Court to be careful how it gave way to the influence of his insolent and disrespectful speech and behaviour.

So after taking him to task for this, and darkly hinting at what they might have done, the chairman said that on the whole they were inclined to suppose, from various circumstances that had not come formally before them, that Israel had laboured under the impression of his boy having received some severe injury from the prosecutor, and therefore they should simply inflict a fine upon him of twenty pounds, and the costs.

Israel drew out a well-filled purse, paid the clerk his demand, and deigning not another word or look to any one, hurried away as fast as he could, the spectators making a lane for him, and gazing in his face with real interest, while one man ventured to say to him as he passed—

' Well done, master, thou'st hit 'em hard!'

' Ha, Lewis, is that thee!' In another minute he was gone, and Mr. Griffith Williams was shaking hands with his brother magistrates, and being now condoled with on his wound, and now congratulated on his verdict, according to the mood and disposition of the speaker.

CHAPTER XVIII.

BY THE SEA MARGE.

By the time Israel Mort had got into the cool air of the street, (which was so refreshing, that almost unconsciously he took off his hat, and stood bareheaded in the soft rain that was falling,) he had forgotten the irritations of his contest and failure with Mr. Griffith Williams—the disappoint-ment of seeing the sweet morsel of revenge or justice snatched from his lips—the loss to his pocket through the fine and the heavy costs—for he already feared some other and greater calamity awaited him.

Prompt as usual in decision, when he had had the opportunity of slowly thinking the matter out beforehand, he, after a brief pause before the court-house, put on his hat; and went not the way he had intended, into the lower part of the town to make inquiries, but straight back to his inn, there to saddle his horse, the ostler being busy, and ride off homewards as fast as his mare could carry him.

He reviewed on the way his late talk with David and his wife, and seemed to feel a certain satisfaction in it, for it showed him there was nothing to be feared in that direction.

Practically he felt sure it was either some monstrous act of stupidity on the part of his wife, or else—Well, he could get no further. The whole business was as inexplicable as it had been injurious.

Could any friend who was driving the same way have called at his house before the man he sent, and persuaded them to go with him, and had the vehicle come to grief in some cross country road that might have been taken to shorten the distance?

Such were the thoughts, fears, and hopes of Israel Mort, who was quite forced out of his usual self by this annoying circumstance, and seemed no longer the same man.

At every solitary house he passed he made

inquiries, but always with the same negative
result, and it was not till he was near home that
he could get the least information.

As he passed the little post office, around
which was congregated some half a score of
gossips, chattering loudly, he noticed there was a
sudden hush, and that all eyes were turned upon
him.

For a moment he fancied they knew something,
and that it was too serious for any one to volunteer
to speak, till he remembered where and on what
business he had been, and that they knew he must
have just come from the court; and he was inclined
to curse his own increasing stupidity and per-
turbation of mind, which disinclined him to speak
to them.

However he stopped, and said carelessly, ' Has
any one seen my wife and son lately? '

There was no answer for a moment, and the
people addressed looked one at another, as if each
suggested somebody else should reply.

' Are you all deaf?' asked Israel, this time with
his old harshness of tone. ' Martin, is that you?'

' Aye, aye, it's me, sure enough ! '

'Is there anything the matter, that they are stricken dumb?'

'Well, we hope not, we hope not. But it seems Bill Barclay met Mrs. Mort and David going towards the sea, at Start Point, about seven o'clock in the morning, and being at work on a bit of allotment land, he naterally expected to see them come back; for, as he says, he knows no other way, except by going a many miles round; but, however that may be, they didn't come back right up to his dinner time. And since then one on us here has just returned from your house, which was locked up, and empty.'

'And is it possible you are all fools enough to think there is anything strange in my wife and son taking a stroll for an hour or two along the sea shore! Start Point, you say?'

'Yes, Master Israel.'

Israel galloped off, never troubling himself about what all those people could have replied, that it was strange, and very strange, his wife and son should take to roaming about the sea shore when they all knew Israel had appointed that very time for them to meet him at Leath court-house.

But he did not forget that appointment as he galloped along, or fail to realise all it suggested. But he stayed his thoughts with the strong hand ; refused to think or speculate, but grimly waited to see what it was he was hurrying to meet.

Leaving him for a brief space, let the reader go back for a few hours and accompany David and his mother on that prolonged visit to Start Point, which so disturbed the kindly spirit of Bill Barclay, while raising potatoes in his allotment ground.

It is one of the brightest, most golden' mornings of the late summer ; a mist has just passed away, and left behind a delicious sparkle in the grass, a crystal clearness in the air.

A ship is seen in the offing, with sail after sail expanding to the crisp but pleasant breeze.

Presently a boat quits the ship for the shore with a couple of men in her, and there waits for a poor weeping woman, whose looks do not belie her case, for she is just parting with her all, her boy, her only remaining child, who does his best to comfort her, and to make her sure he will come back a strong, rich man.

' And then—oh, mother ! who knows ?—perhaps I may marry Nest ! '

The captain is his friend, and will tell her all about him. She will hear of him soon sitting on some high office stool, laughing or crying over her letters, and learning how to begin the life that is to end in his becoming a rich merchant.

Again they embrace, and one of the sailors draws him away and into the boat, while the other, with oars in hand, prepares to start.

He is in, the boat is off, the deed is done that can no longer be undone, but must now be taken with all its consequences.

They wave handkerchiefs to each other incessantly till the ship is reached. The poor mother strains her eyes as if she would read in his face if his purpose falters at the last moment ; but, no— he is too far off for her to judge.

All she can do is to drop on her knees and pray, and so praying and kneeling she moves not, till the mist that grows up in the sea, or the mist that has already filled her own imperfect sight, takes, perhaps kindly, away from her, and for ever, all further power of recognition of the particular ship that holds him. It is lost among the crowd of ships, as he will be lost, she thinks, for her among the crowd of humanity.

She sits down, and buries her face in her hands, and weeps as if she would gladly weep all her life away.

The poor woman's heart seems dying. She could not say so to her poor boy; but what share can she have in his far-off hopes?'

'No, no; if he comes not back till then he will find me in my grave!'

Thus she talks and sobs to herself, and rocks to and fro, and hour after hour passes with her, and still she cannot make up her mind to go home, face Israel's anger, and tell him of David's departure.

One fearful moment came when all things seemed so overwhelming, that before she knew what she was doing, she had risen, and presently found herself looking down into the depths of the sea, longingly, as if they too should take her, as they had taken David.

Suddenly her whole frame thrills and shudders, as a voice like that of doom sounds from behind her.

'Woman, what hast thou done with him? Where is David—my son?'

Summoning up all that remained to her of power to think and speak, and commending her soul to God for what might happen afterwards, she said, gasping for breath, and pausing between every few words—

'He is gone!'

'Gone!'

'He could not—face—the court—and expose all his humiliation. He made a friend of one of the captains who trade here, and this morning the ship has taken him away. Oh Israel—husband— my heart is broken—forgive me—if—'

She could not wait, happily, for the answer he would have given, the blow perhaps he would have inflicted, for she fainted, and Israel had for the next few hours a new case on his hands.

CHAPTER XIX.

DOES MARGARET KNOW?

AMONG those who heard vaguely, and as it were afar off, of the pitiable events just recorded, and which began to fill the whole country side for many miles round with the noise of the ever-increasing strife, there was one man who would gladly have interposed, and at some risk to himself have endeavoured to shame the two combatants into a more Christian-like mood and behaviour.

But unhappily for Rees Thomas's desire to be useful, he is still a prisoner at his lodging; recovering it is true, but so slowly, that even the fact of improvement has been till now doubtful.

And apart from that and the physical depression involved, apart also from the consideration that up to the time of the accident he knew nothing—and after that only heard vaguely of—the attack on David by the Squire, and subsequently, of the retaliation inflicted by Israel, his own mental troubles for once so pre-occupy him that he lacks both the energy and the faith that are necessary to him when embarking in a difficult cause for the service of others.

It saddens him, indeed, with a deeper sadness than he has yet known, to reflect how all the religious earnestness and active impulses for work he has been accustomed to feel seem to have died away.

His weak body seems to him at times like a tenement where angels and saints have communed with his soul, and made their temporary lodging, but which has gradually become so worthless, that the holy and celestial visitants have at last fled, never to return.

It so happened that his first day of assured convalescence was the same as that which witnessed the departure of David. Dr. Jolliffe came in, in a great hurry as usual, felt the pulse, looked at the tongue, asked about the places which had been burned (they no longer needed his looking at them), and having got his answers, said as he put on his hat :—

'I beg you to accept my heartfelt congratulations, Friend Thomas.'

'Indeed!' said the latter, with a gentle but melancholy smile stealing over his face. 'Why?'

'Because you have got rid of me. Good-day.'

And tarrying no further question, away went Dr. Jolliffe; who, if the truth must be told, was a bit of a diplomatist, and perhaps wished to give the collier preacher no opportunity to speak of the delicate questions of fee or reward.

He little guessed what a storm his words raised in Rees Thomas's heart. The time, then, had come! That time he had so much yearned for, even while he so much feared it. Margaret must now be spoken to.

He had been busy when the doctor came in, making notes for a sermon that he hoped some day or other to be permitted to preach; and in which he had got so deeply interested that tears were in the eyes that looked up to see who entered.

Perhaps Dr. Jolliffe had seen these and been moved by them, and found it necessary to cut short his visit, or very much lengthen it—which happened then to be impossible.

When the doctor had gone, Rees Thomas again took up his one and only quill pen, worn down till it could be no longer mended, and endeavoured to go on with his sermon.

Alas! the whole spirit of it had evaporated in these last few minutes. So after vain attempts to get up some fresh energy by reading aloud, over and over again, what he had done, he put down the paper tremulously, and murmured to himself:—

'Why all this hypocrisy? Will it mend the matter in any way? The time has come. She must be spoken to. May the Lord give me courage to resist my own selfish heart, and to think only of what is best for her, which cannot be otherwise than best for me. That is what I must teach myself. That is what I must rely on.'

He began to walk up and down the room; but even in that simple occupation seemed to find a something that troubled the natural simplicity and frankness of his character, and feed the irritability that had grown upon him during the last day or two.

'How many times to-day have I not done this

same thing, for the same object, but without the manliness to avow it, or to wrestle with it, if it is, in truth, a matter to be ashamed of!'

And then, withdrawing the bandage that concealed the part of the face that had been burned, he gazed once more in the little old-fashioned mirror that hung on the wall, and seemed to try to measure the amount and character of the disfigurement.

It was in truth very bad. The wound was quite healed, the skin restored, but frightfully wrinkled, and of so deep-fixed and livid a colour as to preclude all hope of any material amelioration in the future.

He had been so sensitive concerning this matter all through his prolonged illness, that once when Margaret's mother happened to be unable to dress the wound, he positively refused to let it be dressed at all for the time; and this refusal was given so curtly in answer to Margaret's gentle request to be permitted to do it for him, that the poor girl felt at once silenced, and put to shame for her boldness. Consequently, whatever she might have heard from her mother, who was a

taciturn sort of person, and as likely as not to
have said nothing about it of any consequence, she
had never seen what was the effect left behind
after the healing of the burns.

He was angry with himself, as he reviewed this
folly. But for that she would have known, if not
the worst, still enough to be prepared for the
worst. And he would have known how she was
influenced by it, and so have been spared the
fears that tortured him now, when action of some
kind must take place.

Yes, it was quite out of the question his remaining here any longer, unless—but no—he
would not deceive himself—there was—could be
no hope. It was not in human nature for a
young maiden to look with any other feeling
than aversion upon that which he now looked
on. She might love him well enough theoretically
for a time, but—Why he felt he almost abhorred
himself—as if he could no longer recognise himself
—while his eye rested on the features before
him in the glass.

He *must* let her see him in all his deformity.
He must *not* let her see what that would cost him.

Then a few words of kind, and manly, and
Christian explanation, and they would separate in hope, aim, communion of spirit, for
ever, so far as concerned their worldly lives.

Should he take off the wrapping before or after
she should come in? Should he meet her thus
without preparing her beforehand? or should he
give some slight, but sufficient warning?

The shock of the one method might not only be
great for her, but overpower him. Still he
wanted the truth, however painful.

But would such an unexpected revelation fairly
express the truth? Would he not afterwards be
entangling himself in a thousand metaphysical
subtleties, in the endeavour to decide how much
of the emotion she might display would have been
due to natural unsophisticated feeling, telling him
the simple, however bitter truth; and how much
to the unnatural circumstances in which he placed
her by the surprise and suddenness of the spectacle?

He felt heart-sick as he revolved these ideas,
and found no guiding light come, no clear sense
of duty, none of the old fervent inspiration, that

sooner or later was sure to come in prayer, or
after prayer, and set him on his way rejoicing.

Well, he thought at last, those who can't see
their way must feel their way. And then he
knocked with his hand against the wainscot, the
usual signal when he wanted anything.

He fell to shaking like a leaf in the wind, as the
door opened; it was not Margaret, however, who
entered, but her mother.

'Would you ask Margaret to come to me for a
minute?' said Rees Thomas, in as indifferent a
tone as he could assume.

The old woman's face looked brighter than usual
as she said a word or two expressive of her gladness
to hear the doctor's account of him, and then
turned to fetch her daughter.

'Mrs. Doubleday!' It was the earnest voice
of the lodger who thus arrested her steps. He
walked towards her, where she stood against the
edge of the open door, holding the knob in her
hand, took the latter gently from her fingers, and,
very much to her amazement, closed the door as
softly as he could, before again speaking. 'Does
your daughter—does Margaret know how much

I am altered, how disfigured, and I fear for life ? '

' Oh yes, Mr. Thomas ; I told her when you first came home the burn was quite awful, that I was almost overpowered with it ; and it was but yesterday, when I was saying how much better you looked, that she asked me if the marks were going away ; and I couldn't but hold up my hand at her, for supposing such a thing.'

' Thank you; I understand. You acted wisely. Please now let her come to me. I shall not detain her long. I have much to do and think of to-day.'

He then turned, and walked towards his table and sat down, apparently to his sermon, so that she might not tarry, nor again speak to him.

With a kind of half laugh, that yet seemed at any moment ready to change into tears of anguish and despair, he communed with himself, when he saw he was alone,—

' How like children we fret and fume and invent a thousand petty tricks and ingenious subtleties, to do, or not to do, something on which our hearts or our interests are deeply set ; heedless the while how He who disposes of all things is driving us, as the shepherd drives his sheep, to the one and only fold—the truth, as it is in Him, and in His laws for the governance of us all! Oh God, how wouldst thou not laugh at our follies and self-punishings, but that the love which is in Thee—nay, which is Thee—can but pity thy poor erring, lost children, lost but for Thee and thy dear Son!'

Well he knew now what to do. He took off the bandage, and nervously resumed his seat.

Then he rose, stepped hastily to the blind and drew it down a little, to darken the room.

Ashamed of the movement the moment it was made, he drew it up again, and once more sat down.

The door opened, and a soft step was heard inside the room. It paused; then the closing of the door was heard, and the soft step advanced.

Rees Thomas rose, but could not look round; he could only say with an attempt at cheeriness of voice, as he placed a chair for her,

'Come and sit down, Margaret.'

She came, sat down; he turned with a faint

smile on his face, expecting to meet her eyes, and
see in them his own life's happiness or misery at
once revealed—not that he doubted which, but
that he was bound to wait her judgment, not
assume it beforehand.

But he saw eyes cast down, a sweet modest
flush of colour on the face, and a something, he
hardly knew what, of flurry in the dress, especially
about the hair, that seemed to say Margaret had
been striving to make the best use of the brief
moments she had had, between the message and
her obedience to it, to adorn herself.

He felt in the bitterness of his heart he could
almost chide in her the frivolity of the whole sex,
that even when there was nothing they could care
to gain, were still bent on obtaining homage, careless as to the consequences to their victims.

'Margaret!' he said in a deep and agitated tone,
finding she neither spoke nor raised her head,
and seeming, he thought, each moment to become
less capable of doing either.

Then she lifted her eyes; the light was full on
his face, but not so strong but that he was able to
see the change in hers, the sudden painful shrinking

of those blue orbs, and which spread to her whole
frame, the pallor, the confusion of thought and
feeling, and then the consciousness of all she was
revealing to him.

He bore the look, however, as a martyr might
have borne it, in standing before an inexorable
but, so far as his light went, just judge; and seeing
in the eyes of the latter that the verdict was being
given against him.

A moment more, and Margaret could no longer
restrain herself; she wrung her hands, cried aloud
as if for relief, and turning towards the back of
her chair, leaned on it, and gave herself up to the
anguish she could no longer repress.

The unselfish nobility of the man's character
now shone grandly out. Her very distress and
abandonment to it warned him he too must not
also give way. He put aside his own cruel mor-
tification; he thought no more of love; his one aim
and hope was simply to comfort this poor maiden,
and spare her the shock which would by-and-by
come to her on thinking over her behaviour, unless he in the meantime took the sting out of it
by his considerate forethought.

To be as a friend, nay, as a brother to her, and yet to make her understand, without saying so, she had nothing more to fear about his love; that the past was gone utterly; that in a word she was free, and might be sure he would be happy to see her happy, even in marriage with another, should she meet with one worthy of her—these were the things he had to do, alike for her peace and his own.

He waited till he saw the worst of the storm had passed over, then he again breathed gently the word

' Margaret ! '

' Yes,' she responded in a soft melancholy tone, that seemed to express more of a sigh than a word.

' You find me much changed ? '

There was a slight pause before he again heard sounds from the faint lips :

' Oh, what you must have suffered ! '

' We will not dwell on that now. It was not my desire—that is, I should say, I very much desired not to shock you—'

' Oh, Mr. Rees Thomas, don't speak so, don't !

I know you will never be able to forgive me!
I don't deserve it. I am so ashamed of myself.'

'Margaret, you must not say that; you have no
occasion. I owe everything in the world to you,
and your mother—apart, that is, from God's mercies
towards me.'

'And do not I owe more, infinitely more than
that to you; for those mercies you speak of were
of little account to my darkened soul till you made
me see them, understand them, feel them. Oh,
Mr. Thomas, Mr. Thomas'—she stopped, lifted her
eyes to heaven as if seeking light and direction
there to tell her what she ought now to do, then,
before he could arrest her, she had knelt down at
his feet, and with her clasped hands resting on his
knees besought him to think no more of what
had happened just now, and ended by passionately
supplicating him for pardon.

Seeing reasoning was useless, Rees Thomas did
not attempt to explain to her that he felt more inclined to ask pardon from her for even temporarily
defacing the fair prospect of a happy life that lay
before her, but answered in her own spirit,—

'Margaret, I do forgive any pain you may

have given me, as I hope my Maker will forgive me the infinite sorrow I must have caused Him ! '

He then raised her, made her dry her eyes, and sit down again, while he prepared to fulfil that part of his task which remained to him—the hardest of all, the one that had so bowed down his soul, ever since the doctor had released him from his professional bondage.

' Now, Margaret, we must come to business. And I ask you, for my sake, to consider carefully before you speak, and possibly remonstrate ; because I am bound to say this is a matter I alone can decide, and I have made my decision. It was to tell you that, I asked your presence here.'

Whatever Margaret might have thought about his message before she came in, or however deeply she might have been moved since by all that had passed, Rees Thomas did not know, dared not guess, and strove as far as possible not even to think of.

But there was something in her pained look, in the darkening colour of her brow, and in the moistening of her lips with her tongue, as if conscious of the dry, hard tone in which she was about to speak, that betokened at once pride, reserve, and disappointment.

'I shall do my best to satisfy you,' she said; then said no more.

'You see, Margaret, you are young, beautiful, and in all respects one that any man might be proud to win for his wife. You do not think much of these things, I know. But I, your friend, am bound to think of them.'

'You are very good!' said Margaret, almost, he thought, in a tone of irony.

'There can be no harm in my saying that my love for you, while it was received through your great goodness as legitimate, was a sufficient reason for my staying here.'

'Oh indeed!' ejaculated Margaret with an odd kind of smile, while her pretty feet began to beat the floor impatiently, as if she and they knew what all this was coming to, and the sooner it was over the better.

'And then during my illness, when our relations'—he paused in inability for a moment to speak, yet restraining all other show of emotion.

'When our relations?' she repeated; and he felt

her eyes were fixed on his face, and that yet he had to go on.

'When I—I—saw the necessity through my accident for a change in our relations, I could not for the time help myself. But then the world knows that, and so your character cannot suffer.'

'I am glad of that!' said Margaret, and looking almost as if she meant what she said.

'But now, were I to stay on, that would not be so. Enough is known of my—my feelings towards you—what they were, I mean—to make it wrong, decidedly wrong, and in every way disadvantageous to you. Don't you see that? No, do not answer, not now. You will see it by-and-by. And then you will do me justice, whatever now may be your judgment.'

'You, then, wish to leave?'

'Why, to tell you the truth, I have already so far arranged that I have only to speak, and my friend the farmer will be ready to receive me at an hour's notice.'

'I asked you if you wished to leave?'

'You press me unkindly, Margaret!' And he

could not prevent a tear from glistening in his eye,
or her from seeing it.

'Am I, then, to go to my mother, and say,
"Mother, Mr. Rees Thomas is going away, but
doesn't know whether he wishes to go or not?"'

'Margaret, this is cruel.   You know '—

'What do I know?'

'That I love you—aye, a thousand times better
than I ever did before, and that you can no longer
love me.'

The colour was again swiftly mounting to her
cheek; her eyes were full of timid yet joyous light;
if they saw the blemished face, it no longer
troubled them.   There was a brief silence; then in
the lowest, sweetest accents surely ever heard by
mortal ears, she answered,

'Is that true that you first said?'

How could Rees Thomas answer, except from
the ground at her feet, and which he did not
leave till she had assured him of a love far too
deep to be destroyed by the accidents of life?

'Had I been your wife,' she said, with an
infusion of scarlet on her cheeks, to hear her own
lips pronounce the word, 'what would every

honest and true-hearted woman have said of me, if my love had deserted you at your utmost need? Believe me, Mr. Thomas, if your calamity has changed me at all, it is to that which you will have no cause to complain of.'

She leaned down. Their arms, lips, souls met, and for a brief space the lovers knew that the idea of happiness on earth was no fable or dream, but a reality surpassing all imaginings.

And then, when they could speak together again, Rees Thomas warned her of what must happen, thus loving and living together; but she too had foreseen that. And so it was settled that before he began again to work, and exercise his renewed dignity of Deputy, they should be married.

CHAPTER XX.

SUNSHINE.

IT is a custom in Wales to make wedding presents, but which naturally, among very poor people, amount to little more than kindly recognition of the event.

But in the present case the custom led to a result little anticipated by the parties most interested—the pouring in upon them of so many gifts from friends and acquaintances, known or unknown, that they felt themselves suddenly raised from very poor to comparatively very rich people.

Their position was so well known, and his character so highly appreciated, while his personal misfortune and his successful love interested so many among the richer classes, that more than common care was exercised in the choice of the

presents, through a sort of friendly but unacknow-
ledged committee ; of which Mr. and Mrs. Griffith
Williams were the prime movers, and who managed
to make the affair the occasion of a little dramatic
surprise.

The entrance of Mr. Griffith Williams on this
business was too characteristic to be passed over
in silence. Some time before the occurrence of
the injury to Rees Thomas by the Fall in the mine,
he had heard of the quarrel between him and his
employer Israel, and guessed at the cause, their
difference about the beginning work daily at the
mine with morning prayers.

All his own vivid impressions of the conversation overheard by him at the mouth of the pit,
and then the talk with Israel at the bottom, when
it was discovered that the Deputy had rebelled,
and was actually engaged in the very religious
service that had just been forbidden to him—all
this came back to Griffith so freshly, and assumed
such new interest on account of his own bitter
quarrels with Israel, that he suddenly made up his
mind to call at Rees Thomas's lodgings.

He did this in the belief that his only object

was to see if he could promote the interest of a man whom he was so much inclined to esteem ; and taking no account of his secret thirst to hear about the doings at the mine, which he hardly expected would prove creditable to his enemy.

He found not Rees Thomas, the Deputy, whom he sought, but a young woman of striking beauty, and equally striking pallor, who curtsied as he entered, and in reply to the stranger's questions said Mr. Rees Thomas was away, but was expected home.

There was something in her look and in the aspect of the place that sent a chill through the heart of Griffith—she seemed, he thought, literally starving.

By degrees he got her story from her, which was simple and sad enough. She and her mother lived on a bare pittance, saved out of the wreck of former prosperity while her father lived. This they eked out by letting lodgings, and got on very well, when the rent was paid. Now and for a long time Mr. Rees Thomas had lived with them, but more as a friend than a lodger.

For the moment Griffith wondered if the Deputy

took advantage of their good opinion of him to act unworthily. But she went on to say that when in work Mr. Thomas was the most regular of paymasters—in fact often assisting them besides in their need.

After Mr. Thomas—whose name, he observed, she never mentioned except in a tone that implied how deep was her reverence for him—had been discharged by Mr. Israel Mort, he had never been able to obtain for any length of time a similar situation. Everybody spoke well of him, but no one cared to employ him in a post of authority, lest he might make the men insubordinate by his peculiar religious ideas.

'You see, sir, he never was very strong, and mother—and—and his other friends have often begged him not to work as a collier; and he has been so kind as to think of them and not do it. And with the help of the Almighty we have all three managed somehow to get on all through these years; but I do believe his heart is broken at last, for he wrote yesterday, saying he should come back, and ask Israel Mort to let him work among his old comrades as a simple collier, and be content with such pious communion with them as he could get outside the mine.' Mr. Williams paused a moment before he answered her,—

'I am going to see Mr. Jenkyns (a large mine owner of the district) on business, and should I find an opening, will try to do your husband a good turn. He might speak to Israel Mort, which I could not, and so make the business less painful.'

'No, Sir; but thank you all the same. You do not know Mr. Mort. He is one of those men who are always the worse, the more you try to get at them by any but the straight road.'

'Could you lodge a young friend of mine for a few days, if only till your husband's return, if you have not a spare room? He has come down un-expectedly and my house is full.'

'Oh sir, the place is too mean! Yes, indeed, we have a spare bedroom and bed; but, in truth, we have had to part with so many things, that I could not make him comfortable. No, indeed, sir!'

'Will you mind my seeing the bedroom?'

She looked as if she did mind,—that it was

useless and painful,—that he would be sure to
reject it, but led the way up-stairs, like one used
to obedience and disappointment, to a room that
charmed Griffith by the prospect, and by the
remembrance of a fact of which he said nothing
to her, but which was of extreme interest to him
—it was the very room he had occupied while
yet a mere ploughman, earning his fifteen shillings
a week. With companions, or books, he had had
many a happy hour in it, so he insisted it was
all right ; and, as to other matters, why she had
better purchase whatever she felt really indispensable, and they could consider the outlay
afterwards, when they came to the rent.

The artifice was palpable enough, but there was
something so winning in the Squire's countenance
and manner, so determined in his intention that
his friend should stay there, and so grateful to her
in the deference and respect with which he spoke
of Rees Thomas, as if he half suspected on her
part a more than friendly sentiment towards him,
that she felt it difficult to resist ; and when she
thought of the comfort it might be to Mr. Thomas
on his return to find such a man there, one whom

he could talk to, she could not but express a
grateful acceptance.

Griffith put five pounds into her hand, the whole
of which was to be laid out to the best advantage
in provisions and indispensable necessaries, but
laid out at once—the morrow was to be left to
care for itself.

'But if Mr. Thomas be angry with me?' said
the poor girl in alarm. 'He must know you do
this for his sake'—

'And yours,' interjected the Squire.

She coloured a little, but merely remarked,

'He is as proud as he is poor, Sir.'

'He'll forgive you for my sake.'

Strange to say, the young friend, after all, did
not come, though a message from the Squire did,
a day or two later, to apologise; and requesting
her to use what she had bought and what trifle of
money might remain, and to leave him her creditor
for a guest at some future time.

Invaluable had been the help thus rendered;
for, as has already been shown, Rees Thomas did
come back from his unsuccessful search for em-

ployment, and in the lowest depth of poverty and depression.

Remembering these things, and hearing how Rees Thomas had gone to work as a simple collier, and so incurred a life-long disfigurement, he felt he had a greater right than ever to detest Israel Mort for permitting it, and to show his sympathy for the victim. The marriage gave him an opportunity.

When the event began to be talked of among the colliers and the artisans of the neighbourhood, with whom Rees Thomas enjoyed perhaps more respect than popularity, some of his religious acquaintances among the working men began to raise a subscription; but kept the affair strictly private, fearing if he who was to benefit by it heard what they were doing, he would put a decided veto on the business.

One of these friendly artisans called upon the Squire to ask for a contribution. Some talk took place, and it was arranged that the subscription should be vigorously pursued, so that the number of persons contributing might make the compliment the more impressive; and that the money

obtained being brought to him, he would make a
noticeable addition, and so be able to carry out a
little plan he had been contriving, and which he
explained, to the great interest and satisfaction
of the collector.

The marriage feast was to be held at the house
of Morris, Rees Thomas's farmer friend, on the
plea that the cottage of the Doubledays could by
no means accommodate all those who had a right
to be present.

Knowing this, the chief plotter, Mr. Griffith
Williams, with his wife and Nest as delighted on-
lookers playing the part of Chorus to the whole
proceedings, saw that a considerable portion of
the wedding day would be available for the
meditated proceedings. Mrs. Griffith had already
secured a traitor in the household in the person
of Margaret's mother; and through the facilities
and aid she gave, they got drawn up an inventory
of every article of furniture in the place, small or
large, with notes appended showing its state of
preservation, appearance, etc.

They were helped in the concealment, which
was half the charm of the whole affair, by the fact

that on the morning of the day of marriage, the presents that were expected, in accordance with the usual custom, appeared; and were laid out in the one reception room, that where Rees Thomas always sat when writing or studying.

Snowy linen, pretty tea and dinner services, silver tea spoons, &c. &c. &c., were there all duly displayed.

These were examined with real pleasure by Margaret, and calmly approved of by her future lord and master; and so apparently the business ended.

But in truth the best of it had yet to begin. No sooner were they off to church than there came rapidly driving up a large empty cart, with Griffith's groom sitting beside the driver, a broad grin on his face and a paper in his hand.

Guided by this, every condemned article of the household was fetched out, till in fact only a few of the best were left behind. Meantime another vehicle, a roomy van, had come slowly up the steep road, being heavily laden, and accompanied by a couple of helpers, who carefully unloaded it, and displayed to the wondering eyes of the neigh-

bours handsome chests of drawers, always the
central objects in a collier's idea of a well-furnished
home; a bookcase, a tall eight-day clock for the
kitchen, and a little one for the parlour mantel-
piece; new beds and bedding, and chamber furniture; easy chairs, muslin curtains, ornamental
plant-boxes for the windows filled with plants in
full flower, a work table for Margaret fitted with
every convenience, a writing table with drawers
for Rees Thomas; and so on, down to the smallest
articles required even for the humblest use.

All the things belonging to the inside were
rapidly got into place, and then the great clock
was set ticking solemnly, while the flower boxes
were fixed outside the windows; and so all was
ready for the return of the bride and bridegroom.

A gardener had been at work for some hours
in the garden, and made a little Eden of it with
fresh turf, a blooming bed of geraniums edged
with mignonette, and the border weeded, and
newly planted with variegated evergreen shrubs
for winter display.

And thus one of the dullest, though always one
of the cleanest of little cottages, was suddenly

transformed, as by the wave of a fairy's wand, into the brightest, cosiest, most luxurious little home in the world, so far as regarded the wants, wishes, and tastes of the parties concerned.

Fortunately they returned while there was yet sufficient daylight, for the full effect to be seen and appreciated.

Margaret was the first to cry out in a tone of such joyous surprise, that her husband looked at her to see what was the matter.

'Oh don't you see? don't you see?' she exclaimed.

Then he looked towards the home they were approaching, and did see the outward and visible signs of some strange transformation.

The tears sprang to his eyes. Nothing could be sweeter to him under such circumstances than the refined, half-poetic suggestions conveyed by the aspect of the little garden, of the two windows one over the other, belonging respectively to his sitting room and to their bed room, both half embowered in foliage and bloom, and both revealing delicately white curtains within.

But what was the amazement of both on going

into their old familiar place, and finding the changes wrought there!

Alternately laughing and crying, Margaret went from one object to another, calling repeatedly to Rees Thomas to come and look,—

'Oh, do come!' But not waiting for him, she flew on into the kitchen, where her mother was watching with open arms ; then after one rapturous embrace and a fresh gush of bright water drops, she glides upstairs, to her mother's bed room first, to find that too all her womanly heart could desire, then into the bridal chamber, where the first glance was sufficient. She dropped on the nearest chair, put her hands to her eyes, but only to restrain the sense of happiness, almost too great, of a heart far too full.

Where was Rees Thomas all this while?

Sitting down in his new easy chair, in front of his new writing table, opening the drawers on each side, and closing them again, for a minute or two, as if these things were a reality, all the rest a dream.

After that minute or two, he went to his new bookcase, wondering what had become of his

books, but found them all there, with others costly
and most precious—books he had coveted with no
earthly hope of ever possessing, books of infinite
value to one whose education had been all his own
work, and through a thousand difficulties; therefore of most imperfect character.

But he did not even touch these now. He
wanted his pocket bible; and was half in alarm
lest that, like so many other of his shabby household gods, should have been improved out of
existence. But no; he found it, and went back,
sat down, and began to read in it; but evidently
did so as a question of soul-discipline, of pious
gratitude, of desire to tread down under feet by
its aid those swellings of the heart that threatened
to carry him he knew not whither, as he thought
of those who had so changed his home to-day.

But who were they?

He hears, as if in answer to a question that he
had only put to himself in silent communion,
sounds of stifled laughter; then he hears Margaret's
voice, then an opening of doors, and a rush of
sounds and of feet; and presently he is surrounded by a group of familiar faces, conspicuous

among whom are Mr. and Mrs. Griffith Williams,
and little Nest, her excitement bubbling over in
silvery peals of mirth. There too is his farmer
friend, who had been kept in ignorance, till the last
hour or two, of the little plot. And there is Dr.
Jolliffe, who, with a bright smile and a genial clasp
of hands, has to hurry away.

And then came in two of Mr. Williams's servants
with trays bearing the contents of certain hampers
they had just unpacked in the kitchen; and though
neither Rees Thomas nor Margaret could eat or
drink anything, no one found them out; the supper
was to everybody else a most enjoyable one.

As to the Squire, the occasion seemed to deve-
lope quite an unknown side of his character. Without putting off the gentleman, he was so amusing,
sympathetic, jovial, and frank, that it was hardly
possible to resist the belief he had erred in accepting solitude when dissatisfied with his reception
in the society he had sought to belong to.

One thing alone jarred on his enjoyment of the
evening. In devising the scheme that had been
so well carried out, he had remembered not only
the higher social standing that a man like Rees

Thomas was entitled to, but also his own great desire to show Rees Thomas how indignant he felt at Israel's brutal tyranny, and how much he admired the stand he made against him. And then he meant to offer his own aid in obtaining employment elsewhere.

But when he spoke on the subject to Rees Thomas, at the moment the little impromptu party was breaking up, he was disconcerted and excessively annoyed to discover, what he had not previously known or suspected, that the two were again friendly, the prayers about to be resumed, under Rees Thomas as Deputy.

After that he could' not touch on the question of David, as he had intended. And he took leave of Rees Thomas, with an effort to keep up the cordiality of the evening, that only told himself how the doings of the day had suddenly lost all their flavour, and that the sooner he forgot them the better.

Rees Thomas in part saw this, and grieved, but it was no time to speak, and he had too much cause for happiness to be willing to mar it now.

When all but himself, his wife, and her mother

had gone away, they knelt down in prayer; and
Rees Thomas poured forth all the emotion and
gratitude of his heart for the past, all his aspirations for their common future, in language at once
so homely and so touching, that it was accompanied by tears and sobs throughout, but most
happy ones; and when he ended there came from
each of the listeners in one fervent word, all they
cared to say, or desired,

'Amen! Amen!'

CHAPTER XXI.

SHADE.

THE work of reparation of the mine now went on so vigorously, seemed so thoroughly to occupy Israel's whole soul, as to leave him neither time nor inclination to attend to what all his neighbours had supposed must prove an overwhelming calamity, the departure of David, to seek his way in the world, alone and friendless.

After the first shock of his violence, Mrs. Mort had found him hear her account of the business with more patience and good feeling than she had dared to hope for. Indeed, as her prostration of mind and body became plain to him, he ministered to her by kindly acts, though he did not use kindly words.

Once only he broke through the impassive front

he had maintained after the first few hours of knowledge, and said to her,

'David will probably come back. If so, and he says anything at all satisfactory as regards the future, I shall wash out the past as I wipe out these memoranda from my slate.' And with a sponge he cleaned the slate carefully before again speaking. 'But I hereby warn you never to mention his name to me again, till he does. From this time I also wipe out and make clean my mind of him, as this slate is clean—aye, that I will, even to the very recollection of him, for any or all practical purposes!'

What could she say or do, but just what she had always to say or do—submit?

And then Israel went to work as if the very attempt of circumstances to impede him for the moment made him only move on with redoubled force afterwards.

The day came, so long looked for by Mrs. Jehoshaphat, the day of her visit to see at work all the labourers in the busy hive of industry that her money alone now maintained, while she could

see them—that is, while the works were going on
at the surface, or were, to some extent, visible
from it.

Everything regarding the transit, from her eyrie
on the mountain ledge down to the mine-mouth,
was managed to her entire satisfaction, and with
no perceptible jar to her nerves, or injury to her
aged and weak frame.

But then she was in such spirits, that it would
have required a somewhat rude jar or decided
injury to affect her. Never was there a woman
with whom the value, or comfort, or happiness of
the passing hour, depended more on the quality
of the existing mood, which too was usually passing, even while one gazed on its manifestations or
effects.

She had dressed herself in gorgeous attire : a
crimson velvet robe, seal-skin jacket, and swans-
down boa round her neck; a bonnet indescribable
for size, the variety of its colours, and the rarity
of the pendent flowers that hung from it, and
which the most skilful botanist would have found
it difficult to assign to their right place in the
Linnæan, the natural, or any other system. She

wore yellow kid gloves, and rings over them on every finger. She was the queen of the day, and felt quite equal to all demands for queenliness of costume and behaviour that could be made upon her.

They carried her in an easy chair, taken from her own room, down the steep, winding, and dangerous descent, at the bottom of which a Bath chair awaited her; and in this she was drawn gently and carefully over the inequalities of the way, towards the mine.

The moment she was within sight of the place, her ears were greeted by a great shout, and her eyes, by the display of waving hats and hand-kerchiefs, and gay flags, and she soon discovered what previously she had neither known nor sus-pected, that Israel had passed the word round among the colliers, and the colliers' wives and sweethearts and daughters, that there was to be a bit of a public ceremony at the laying of the first stone of the masonry around the pit mouth, and that he wished a good reception to be given to Mrs. Jehoshaphat, who was coming.

The cries of welcome from the voices of the multitude, who, in their holiday costume, and with such a mingling of the sexes presented a some- what picturesque appearance, was immediately afterwards taken up by an amateur band playing an inspiriting march.

Israel advanced to meet her, to receive a most cordial shake of the hand, and to see the tears of pride in the old lady's eyes, as she said—

'This is a surprise, Israel Mort. Ah! I see you have learned to sound the depths of the old fool's weakness, and, shall I say, to take advantage of her?'

'Say it by all means, ma'am, if you think it, or if it will comfort you!'

'But, Israel, what do you think, man?' exclaimed the old lady with a joyous laugh. 'The doctor actually and positively forbade this expedition, and said he washed his hands of the business altogether, if I did. And here I am, feeling so well, that I can't but ask which is the biggest old woman, Dr. Jolliffe or me?'

'Well ma'am, I am sorry to hear so decided an opinion from the doctor; but however, as you say, here you are, and it must be our business to take care you shan't be able to say so for long.'

'Oh, you mean to send me quickly back, do you? That'll depend, Israel Mort, that'll depend!'

He wasted no time in contention, for he knew that could not benefit her now. So he set the artisans to work again, whom her coming had interrupted.

While he was thus engaged, she turned eagerly and impatiently round, now in this direction now in that, to see here the great stack of props for the interior, there masons at work on the masonry for the exterior; here the yawning gulf of the new shaft, already far advanced to completion; there the similar gulf of the old one, with the cage incessantly going up and down with materials; here the long array of gigantic beams, to form the spears of the new pump; there an enormous pile of bricks, for particular portions of the roofing below; here empty waggons going away, there loaded waggons coming up.

When Israel rejoined her, she could not but notice a certain gravity in his face, which she had by this time learned to read so well, as to know that if it ever did express anything particular it was because its owner chose that it should, and indeed compelled it to do so.

' What's the matter, man? Pray don't dash my spirits to day. You can't have any news to tell me that must be told now, or that can be so very important as to matter when it's told.'

' No, ma'am, but I want to say a word and then it's done with, and I will wait your good pleasure.'

' What is the word ? '

'This: you have provided me with money freely, handsomely, as I wanted it, and I didn't like to ask you to put into the bank, once for all, enough for the job.'

' Of course you didn't like to ask me, nor should I have done it if you had.'

'Suppose, ma'am, anything were to happen while things are in this state ? '

' Happen ! to me ? '

' Yes, ma'am.' Mrs. Jehoshaphat's face visibly paled, and the pallor increased to such a deadly hue, that for the moment Israel feared he had all unconsciously touched a dangerous chord of fear in her heart. But when she spoke, which she could not do for a little time on account of her ever-present enemy, the cough, it was to pour out a torrent of anger and almost of imprecations at him who had first suggested the visit.

He stood quiet, submissive under the storm, saying nothing to irritate her, trusting to what he had before seen of her good sense, which always came to her aid before she had very much committed herself. So it proved now. She stopped, and for a while there was a spell of grim silence. Then she said—

' I suppose what you are driving at is, that if I die before these works are finished, you may not be able to get the money to go on, is that it? '

' Exactly, ma'am! But I hope you see that if you kindly take steps to prevent that, you won't live a year, or an hour the less; perhaps indeed, by making me easy, I may do a little to—'

' Right! right! confound you, Israel Mort, you are always in the right! Can't you manage to get at what you want, and let me, for once in the way, when we differ, seem to have the best of the argument? '

' I'll try, ma'am ! '

She burst out laughing as she said—

' I know you will. Here's my hand. Come to me to-morrow, and you shan't leave till the proper sum is arranged and provided, so that whatever "happens" as you say, you shall be safe.'

' Say the mine, ma'am ! It's that that I want to see safe.'

' Very well, and mind in future, when one gets to my age and state, they don't like to be told suddenly of what may "happen." It's an ugly word, and it shook me.'

' I am really sorry, very sorry ! But you don't feel any the worse now I hope ? '

' No, I think not, but I shan't wait for the laying of the stone.'

' Surely you will. It'll soon be over.'

' Very well,' she said, with an air of lassitude, while still striving to look round and recover her interest in the spectacle. ' Are they ready ?

' They will be in a very few minutes. I will quicken them. There shall be no fuss, only a few words, a good hurra, and there an end.'

But he had not moved twenty yards away, before he heard a scream; he turned and saw Mrs. Jehoshaphat's head lying on her breast, and shaking about as if its owner had lost all power of self-control.

He ran back, raised the aged head, tore off the bonnet, with its blaze of garish colours, and threw it on the ground. The movement loosened her long grey hair, which floated about in the wind. He saw she had fainted. He shouted for brandy or anything else that might be instantly obtainable. A collier's tea-can was handed to him as the only available thing. He tried to pour some down her partly open mouth, heard a gurgling of the throat, and all was over. Mrs. Jehoshaphat was dead.

CHAPTER XXII.

ISRAEL SURPRISED.

PEOPLE no longer talked of the fortunate Israel. The departure of David, and the death of his only supporter were blows sufficiently severe to have damaged even an older reputation for good luck than Israel Mort's. It soon became known that Mrs. Jehoshaphat had died without a will, and without making provision for the completion of the extensive works of reparation at the mine, and the consequences to Israel stared everyone in the face.

How would he act now? Where would he get capital? These questions naturally led to the further enquiry, What would become of Mrs. Jehoshaphat's property in the mine, and would the heirs carry out her intentions regarding it?

Consumed from this moment with secret and

ceaseless anxiety, Israel preserved what in any
other man would have been called a cheerful
aspect; was as exact and exacting, as methodical
and observant as ever. Judging from his behaviour one would say no thought ever crossed his
mind of interruption to his government; and therefore that no man in his employ need fancy he
might relax in his labours, or be less careful of
expenditure, or slacken in the precautions, now
more than ever required for safety.

And now he found how invaluable were the
services of Rees Thomas. The man's face, in spite
of its disfigurement, seemed to have become trans-
figured with happiness. He grew stronger too;
more physically able to help Israel.

Thus it happened that the latter found it possible to be away from the mine day after day,
sometimes for nearly a week together, while he
was making herculean efforts to raise funds for
the ever-recurring fortnightly wage-days, and to
negotiate for the introduction of a sleeping partner, who would buy out Mrs. Jehoshaphat's heirs;
the Deputy, the while, in no respect departing
from his ordinary humble quietude

Whenever Mort returned from these wearying and depressing expeditions, he had only to go to the mine to draw new spirit and hope from the sight, for he found all things moving on exactly in the grooves he had made, and with no loss of force, but on the contrary with a very decided gain ; which came unexpectedly on Israel, and with most important consequences at a critical time.

To get the largest possible quantities of coal out of the mine in the shortest possible period, was the problem that had to be solved ; and it was on the character of the solution that depended Israel's chance of obtaining enough ready money to hold his ground unassisted till he could secure external relief, and, what was equally important, at a reasonable price.

He had, of course, stopped at once, on Mrs. Jehoshaphat's death, all the new works ; and confined himself to doing just so much, and no more, to the old ones, as would enable the ordinary business of coal-winning to go smoothly on.

But this would have been insufficient, and he must have succumbed, but for the ingenuity and vigour of Rees Thomas; who without any confidential talk with his employer, understood exactly where the shoe pinched, and how best to ease it; and so managed matters with the men, that a sudden and large increase was made in the weekly produce of the mine, and time given to Israel to realise its value before he had to pay the necessarily increased earnings of the labourers.

He needed some such comfort, for he was again to be painfully surprised.

He often wondered how it was he could get no answer to his repeated applications to the solicitors who had the administration of Mrs. Jehoshaphat's property, and whom he had asked to continue the works she had begun, and pledged herself to continue; but one day, when overcome with fatigue, and perhaps (though he would have hardly owned the fact even to himself) feeling to lose heart over the ceaseless harass of the fortnightly wage days; he went into a public house, for the first time for a very long period, and called for a glass of ale, and bread and cheese.

Taking out his notes of people to call on who owed money to the mine owners; or who might

become customers and be willing to pay at once
tempted by liberal discount ; he, after a brief
glance, put them by impatiently, and called for
a newspaper.

Turning it over and over with that listless
look that shows how little one thinks of it,
news, politics, and advertisements being about
equally unattractive to a man engrossed in fighting
a terrible social battle of his own ; suddenly his
eye brightens and flames, as if roused by some
startling incident; he at once stretches out the
paper mechanically on the table, and standing, and
leaning over it, reads with slow deliberate self-
torture a long and showily displayed advertisement of the sale by auction of his own mine !

Having once read it all through he paused, and
putting his hands over his eyes to shut out the
light, and whatever else might disturb him, he
remained for some minutes in that attitude, in
intense thought, his body rocking a little to and
fro, and his feet rising and falling with the movement.

Then he again glanced over the salient points
of the advertisement, half mechanically, reading

of the valuable leasehold colliery known as Cwm Aber—railway sidings to the port—fourteen seams of coal of the aggregate thickness of fifty-seven feet or thereabout—coal well known in steam coal markets, and on the Admiralty list—one shaft in working order, another partly built—royalty moderate—lease renewable on moderate terms—machinery in good working order—cottages, stabling, and other buildings, &c. &c. &c. Also the very valuable rent-charge on the mine of three thousand a year, amply secured, and payable before any division of profits. 'May be inspected on application to the Agent, Mr. Israel Mort, or Messrs. Johnes and Dynevor, solicitors, Leath.'

'To Mr. Israel Mort, eh?—Agent!—' he said aloud as he put the paper in his pocket, forgetting it was not his own. Then, after slowly finishing his meal, his first resolve was to go at once to the solicitors named in the advertisement, and demand by what right they proposed to sell the mine, instead of selling simply Mrs. Jehoshaphat's shares.

It may be said at once, he had a great misgiving that somehow or other he had trusted too much to his own sagacity in his final arrangements with the old lady ; and for that very reason he took the shortest, but possibly least prudent course in going at once to the enemy's camp, and risking the display of the strength or weakness of his position.

Messrs. Johnes and Dynevor were both in the room to which he was admitted, and appeared quite amused by his question, and instead of replying to it, Mr. Johnes asked,—

'You were a collier in the mine, I think?'

'Yes,' said Israel, measuring the speaker with his eye, sternly.

'And then Deputy and Overman?' chimed in Mr. Dynevor.

'Yes,' said Israel, studying the new querist's face in the same hard, imperturbable fashion.

'Then pray how did you find the means to pay for that third share in the mine, which you now demand?' again asked the same gentleman.

'I don't demand anything of the kind. I ain't such a fool!' said Israel.

'What then?' was the supercilious response of Mr. Johnes, while the partners exchanged a laugh.

Out of which they were unpleasantly shaken,

however, when Israel's fist came down on the
morocco-covered writing-table with such violence
as to set the inkstands and papers dancing, and
to cause the virgin purity of the latter, including
some very important documents just going away, to
receive very serious stains.   Nor were his accompanying words calculated to restore their compla-
cent equability.

'I came here to demand by what right you
propose to sell my property without my consent.
And if you don't choose to answer me, an injunction shall, before many hours are passed.'

The two gentlemen again exchanged glances,
in which no particle of fun or humour was visible.
Something was wrong evidently.   So Mr. Dynevor,
after a brief pause, said in a grave tone,

'We don't at all understand, Mr. Mort.   We
have been told by the heirs that you have no
rights whatever; that you had simply planted yourself on the old woman ; but that when she went
you went too, as far as they or their interests were
concerned.'

Israel laughed, actually laughed, before beginning to rummage his capacious pockets, from

which he drew a paper, one he now always carried about with him, as needing on occasion to be shown to possible future partners.

It was simply a copy of his deed of partnership. This he placed before the two gentlemen, who, laying their heads together, began at once hurriedly to read it.

Israel quite enjoyed the spectacle their faces presented, lengthening and darkening every instant, not because they cared who were, or who were not, the true owners, but to see they had been so played with; and had, in consequence, made such asses of themselves before an acute, strong fellow like Israel Mort.

A half-stammered apology was offered and accepted; and so far. Israel was victor. The two gentlemen undertook at once to modify the advertisement, acknowledging his third share. And Israel undertook to let them see the original agreement, 'a mere form,' they added, for satisfaction.

But his victory was to be dashed with a serious reverse.

Messrs. Johnes and Dynevor showed him—

and it was his turn then to be surprised and to look a little blank—a passage in the will of Mr. Jehoshaphat, in which he had anticipated that Mr. Griffith Williams might wish to dispose of the mine; and had absolutely forbidden it, without the consent of his wife, should she be living, or of her heirs after her death; his object being the better to guard the charge upon the mine in her favour of three thousand a year, which she was to enjoy and have the power to bequeath. It would seem from this, Mrs. Jehoshaphat, who was never remarkable for consistency, still desired to keep the mine in the family; whether in cynic enjoyment of its dubious value, or from the desire that they should do what he had declined doing, put their shoulders to the wheel as capitalists, and drag its notorious ill-fame out of the mud, who shall say?

'So you see, Mr. Mort, nobody but Mrs. Jehoshaphat's heirs can sell the mine as a whole,' remarked Mr. Johnes, after a decent pause.

'And does that prove that *they* can, if I resist?' shrewdly asked Israel. 'Remember I became proprietor *with her consent*, when the mine was purchased *with her consent*, from Mr. Griffith Williams. So again I ask can the heirs sell without me ? '

' We think so, and should fight if our view was legally obstructed.'

' And so ruin the property for both sides ? '

' Well, that does happen at times ! ' said Mr. Johnes, with a smile, to which his partner assented by a loud laugh.

' We may as well tell you that the late Mrs. Jehoshaphat has left a very large property indeed, inherited of course from her husband ; that the heirs are thus able to spend money freely ; and that they have taken a particular dislike to you— why we don't pretend to say; but it's as well you should see how the matter stands.'

Some conversation now took place on the prospects of the sale, which the solicitors thought looked gloomy. Even before seeing him they had not expected a very good price, but now if they were to offer only two-thirds of the property, they doubted if they should have a decent bid. Was he willing to let the whole be sold, and take his third in money from the proceeds, and then arrange afterwards as he could with the buyer?

No; Israel was not willing. He knew that mine, and he knew no other. It was his lawful wife, and he had no notion of divorce.

Seeing no more was to be got out of them, Israel went away; saying to himself, 'That game won't do for me, nohow, and so I must bide the worst, and see what the auction brings forth.'

CHAPTER XXIII.

THE DAY OF SALE.

NOT for many years could the oldest frequenters of the sale room of Mr. Lewis Williams at Leath remember an occasion that excited so much interest, or brought together so large an assemblage of spectators, and possible buyers, as the putting up to auction of the mine of Cwm Aber.

The great wealth of Mr. Jehoshaphat was only just beginning to be known, his wife's illnesses and oddities having concurred to delay administration to the will. This was one source of the public interest. Another was the critical position of Israel Mort, between the dead partner and the living partners, which led to frequent comment and speculation. A remark made by one person to another as the crowd was gathering, and which speedily was repeated throughout the room as a good thing, fairly illustrated the general feeling :—

'Oh, depend on it, Mort's got somebody, as rich and as foolish as Mrs. Jehoshaphat, to buy; and we shall see him emerge before long, most likely, as owner of half the estate, with a lien on the remainder.'

But there was yet another attractive feature of the sale,—the possible appearance in the room of Mr. Griffith Williams. Nay, who could tell, people asked, with a smile, but he would be the buyer, out of pure love for Israel, and so shake hands, and be friends once more?

This was but gossip, but the gossip reached Israel Mort, and affected him more deeply than he would like to have been conscious of.

That was just the one and only thing that he could see in the distance, of the nature of a calamity, likely to enhance his present dangers and troubles.

And Mr. Griffith Williams was the very first person he set eyes on when he entered the auctioneer's room, and who saw him enter ; and, Israel fancied, with a half smile, that was immediately repressed.

The gossips had only done justice to Israel's aims and energy. He had not idled away the interim betwixt the appearance of the advertisement and the day of sale. After many refusals from neighbouring coal-owners whom he knew personally, and after employing numerous agents, whom he stimulated by the promise of a large bonus in the event of success, he found at last a mining agent, who had received a commission from a client, a Mr. Colman, to inquire into the state and property of the mine, with a view to investment.

Could he see Mr. Colman? It was feared not, but he had said he should be at the auction.

Israel knew Mr. Colman to be a man of ample capital and estimable character, and that he was a busy man, far too busy to think of managing Cwm Aber himself.

So he sat down at once where he was, wrote for some hours, and then handed to the agent a paper which he said would tell Mr. Colman all he wanted to know, and the accuracy of which he guaranteed.

And with that Israel Mort was obliged to be content, hardly knowing whether he was dealing with a friend or foe.

But on the very morning of the sale a note had reached Israel from Mr. Colman authorising him to bid on his, Mr. Colman's responsibility, ten thousand pounds for the two-thirds share held by the heirs, and another ten thousand for the charge on the mine.

He proposed also to be there himself in time to bid, but gave Israel power in case of accidental hindrances.

Thus armed Israel entered the auction room and took up a position where he could be sure to see every glance of the auctioneer, and be able to make him in return see or hear any sign or sound he might make.

The critical question for him was whether or no Mr. Colman would get the mine for ten thousand pounds, a miserable and utterly inadequate price, or whether anybody would drive the price up beyond that sum.

What if by any possibility Griffith Williams had got to know of this arrangement? Would it not stimulate him, if he were at all open to buy, to venture a figure beyond the ten thousand, believing that some one else would also advance on this, and so free him while shutting out Israel and his supporter? Or even if the mine were knocked down to the Squire, he might still be content, knowing as he did it was worth so much more than it was likely to fetch.

But Israel Mort had in any case one great consolation: the higher the sum obtained, the larger would be the estimated value of his third share.

The auctioneer, who was fond of his own eloquence, described in glowing characters the value of the mine, and its almost illimitable capabilities, which he illustrated by figures and statistics that startled Israel, who seemed to recognize in them a sort of reflection of his own statement to Griffith Williams, during their former negociations.

But he was re-assured, as he remembered that if Griffith Williams had helped the heirs to make the best of the property by furnishing such particulars it must be quite clear that he could not intend himself to buy.

The auctioneer proposed to begin with sixty thousand pounds, but finding no one tempted to speak, then descended by bold steps of ten thousand each till he had got only one ten thousand left behind to work by.

A voice in a far off corner now called out

'Five thousand!'

Israel craned his neck round and rose on tiptoes to discover the bidder, and recognized the voice as that of an agent, one employed by him, but who had failed. So Israel had not the least idea what the bid meant, having had no recent communication with him.

Would Mr. Griffith Williams now strike in? Israel could not but look, with that iron face of his, towards his enemy, who stood by the auctioneer, but made no sign.

'Six thousand!' said Israel, on the part of Mr. Colman, who had not yet arrived, and for whom he looked with anxiety, not as doubting the authority given to him but that Israel knew enough of human nature to know that if Mr.

Colman were himself bidding, and was forced up
to his mark, he would probably, at the last moment, strain a point, and go farther than he had
said he would.

'Seven thousand!' called out the agent.

'Eight!' said Israel, but only after as long a
pause as he dared, for he wanted to stretch out
the time, and so let Mr. Colman come to rescue
him from his unknown foe.

'Nine thousand!' promptly replied the agent.

Again delaying as long as possible, but watching
the auctioneer's eye the while, as sharply as if he
thought it possible he might be in collusion with
those who seemed bent on defeating his plans,
and so suddenly let his hammer fall, he called out
with as steady a voice as if he were prepared for
any number of advances yet, while knowing it
was in fact his last bid—

'Ten thousand!'

He began to breathe again, as he found this
time his bid was followed by a deep silence.

In vain the auctioneer recapitulated all the
' points' of the bargain offered, and expatiated on
the certain wealth it would secure to an enter-

prising speculator; no one advanced, and Israel began to look somewhat sternly at the speaker, as if asking whether he was not exceeding the usual etiquette of the institution by delaying to strike.

Mr. Griffith Williams's voice was now for the first time heard speaking aloud. He remarked in his usual courteous and gentlemanly way, that probably there might be some present who would prefer to bid for the mine and the charge upon it, as one lot. And he should not object to begin with an offer of fifteen thousand pounds.

The auctioneer, after a pause to see if anybody objected, accepted the suggestion; for which, indeed, he did not seem unprepared.

Israel felt the ground gliding from under his feet, but restrained all tokens of emotion as he said simply—

'Sixteen!'

'Thank you! Sixteen thousand pounds only are offered, gentlemen. Sixteen thousand only for that which on my conscience I believe is capable of returning at least sixteen thousand a year!'

'Seventeen!' said Mr. Griffith Williams, and it was evident his face and voice were influenced by secret and strong feeling which he could no longer restrain. He and Israel were once more face to face, and dealing with mightier weapons for weal or woe, than horsewhips, or the documents of petty litigation.

Looking in vain for Mr. Colman and trying now different tactics, Israel at once responded boldly—

'Eighteen!'

'Nineteen!' almost shouted Mr. Williams.

The critical moment had now come indeed. Israel's next must be his last bid, his last chance of influencing the future partnership.

A bold thought occurred to him.

'Is it understood, Mr. Lewis Williams,' he asked, 'that the management of the mine is vested in me?'

'Oh, Mr. Mort, we can't go into such matters here! Any advance on nineteen thousand pounds? Going for nineteen!'

'One moment, sir,' thundered Israel's voice through the room, 'one moment! I have not done bidding. But I wish you to take note that I here publicly avow my right to sole management, and that, whoever be the purchaser, I will defend that right to the last!

'Any advance?   Going, going—'

'Twenty thousand!' cried Israel, and so loud as to make it impossible that there should be any cry of too late!

The auctioneer looked at Mr. Williams, but he shook his head.

Israel's blow had told.

Then friends began to whisper to the Squire, and there was quite a commotion among the group amid which he stood.   The auctioneer, instead of again calling for an advance, and threatening with his hammer to knock the property down to the last bidder, began leisurely to cut open and suck an orange.

Then advancing to him, Mr. Griffith Williams and he whispered together, and continued to do so, till Israel interrupted them :—

'Let's have all fair and above board, Mr. Lewis Williams, or the sale may be vitiated.'

Appearing to treat the remark with unconcern, Mr. Lewis Williams did however at once stop the talk, and resume his hammer.

And then seeing that the commotion had ceased, and that Mr. Griffith Williams had evidently made up his mind one way or the other, the auctioneer, carefully not looking at him, began once more to ask :

'Any advance on twenty thousand, gentlemen ?

'Twenty-one,' said Griffith Williams.

Israel looked despairingly round once more for his backer, Mr. Colman, but looked in vain.

'Any advance on twenty-one thousand pounds? I shall not dwell!' And he did not. Barely giving Israel time to bid, if he had intended to do so again, the hammer fell, and the result was announced :—

'Purchaser—Mr. Griffith Williams.'

CHAPTER XXIV.

TAKING POSSESSION.

ISRAEL was not long left in doubt as to the special thoughts that had moved Griffith Williams in the last moments of the bidding, first to give it up on hearing Israel's statement that he was permanently manager, and then suddenly to return to his first intention, after the brief discussion with his friends.

The very next day that gentleman appeared at the pit mouth, accompanied by the said friends and by his solicitors, no longer the pettifogging Mr. Croft, of whom Griffith had got ashamed, but Messrs. Johnes and Dynevor ; whose presence, when made known to Israel, explained in part the excellent understanding he had seen to exist between the auctioneer acting for the heirs, and his former employer.

Israel was at home at the time, unaware of the honour intended him; and in consequence the solicitors proposed to send down for Rees Thomas the Deputy, and say to him what they had come to say.

But a sharp collier's lad, who had already got a kind of knowledge of the bad feeling between his present employer and his former employer, stepped out of the staring group of black faces relieved by whites of eyes, who looked on with wonder at the gentlemen's doings, and ran as fast as he possibly could to Israel's house, and burst in upon Israel and his wife sitting at an early dinner with the intimation—broken by gasps for breath—

' Oh sir—please Mr. Mort—there's Mr. Griffith Williams and a lot of other gentlemen at the pit mouth, and I don't know what they ain't a going to do ! '

' Who sent you ? '

' Nobody but myself—please.'

' Good lad ! Put that shilling in your pocket, and we'll have a talk about you and the mine another time. Now can you run back, even faster than you came? '

The lad grinned—and though still panting, said he didn't know he was sure, he had come pretty fastish.

'Well, quick as you can! Say to Mr. Griffith Williams I am coming, then find Rees Thomas; if he's below, let the cage go down with you, to the stoppage of everything else, and tell him to resist with all the force at his command any attempt to descend.'

'I will, sir.'

'Off then! I shall be not many minutes after you.'

The lad, benefited by even so temporary a rest, flew along, revelling in dreams of what this run was to bring him.

Meantime the gentlemen had not been without occupations to amuse them. They had sent for Mr. Rees Thomas; who, after they had waited a long while, replied by the same messenger, he could not possibly attend upon them for an hour or so, and had privately warned their messenger to seek his master instantly.

The gentlemen, however, had not thought proper to wait for his re-ascent. The assembled party marched in a body into the little counting-house, where it was with difficulty they found convenient standing room; and Mr. Williams and the solicitors began to rummage the table and drawers and cupboard for books of accounts and papers, while the others looked on approvingly.

Nothing the searchers did find seemed to meet their exact want; so they put all back, and at last made a dead stand before a locked desk.

'The books we want are there,' said Mr. Griffith, pointing at it; and looking heated while striving to appear calm.

'Probably;' said one of the solicitors, and turned away to whisper to his partner, who was heard to reply to some enquiry or suggestion—

'Certainly not! Too dangerous! Too violent! Not to be thought of for a moment.'

But Griffith Williams heard and understood, and accepting the fact that one of the two shared his own thought, said,

'Let it be broken open!'

Messrs. Johnes and Dynevor looked at one another, and respectfully began to explain that—

But their client was no longer accessible to

reason. He had got a notion that if only he took possession of the two books he had learned Israel himself kept, containing, the one, a daily record of all cash payments and all cash receipts, and the other of the Dr. and Cr. accounts of all who dealt with the mine, he would be able to paralyse action on Mort's part, fortify his own claim, by sheer strength of possession, to the entire management; and. as having the worst possible opinion of the man's honesty, perhaps find out something, he hardly knew what, that might enable him to show up his late manager as the vilest of rogues.

Turning suddenly upon the men of law, Griffith said, with concentrated feeling, 'If you won't break it open, I will.'

As they hesitated—for they were alike unwilling to offend against law and decency on the one hand, and against so valuable a client on the other—he caught up a half rusty screw-driver that lay temptingly near; and, in spite of the earnest protestations of his advisers, but stimulated by the partisan spirit of his friends, he in a moment drove in the iron, and forced up the lid; and there were the two books that had been described to him—

one a pocket ledger in green leather, the other a sort of big ciphering book in rough calf.

It was at this moment the messenger returned from the depths below with Rees Thomas's reply, saw what had been done, and saw Griffith Williams pocket the ledger, while he began with eager suspicion to study the bigger cash book, by laying it open on the table.

Getting no reply, the man hastened away to Israel, and almost immediately met the boy running as if for dear life, and who shouted, Mr. Mort was coming directly.

The messenger, however, went on till he met his employer, some half mile further on, and made known the very serious news of what he had seen.

One moment only for thought did Israel give himself, with eyes fixed on the dead fern below his feet, then said,

'Fetch Crump. He is at home; I saw him only a little while ago. Tell him I need his aid instantly at the mine. Say, too, I have secured for him that which he wanted. He must bring his staff of office. Stop; tell every night-shift man you meet on your way, or find lolling about, to hurry instantly to the mine; that I want help at once!'

Away went the messenger, a man chosen by Rees Thomas for the occasion, and who proved worthy of it. For within ten minutes after Israel himself reached the mine, he saw at least a dozen colliers running towards him; and beyond them he saw approaching, and already near, the constable Crump.

Before going into the counting-house he was thus able to draw hastily together behind one of the buildings quite a little band of men who he knew would obey him. He bid them remain there till he whistled; then burst in and sweep everybody out they found inside, using as little violence as possible, but 'doing the job.'

'Ay, ay, master; we understand,' said one of the foremost.

Thus prepared Israel left them, emerged from the shelter of the building, advanced to the office door, and went in; the gentlemen who blocked it up giving way, and staring hard at him, as if to ask how he liked the look of the business now.

Griffith Williams was at the moment engaged, as before described, leaning over the cash book and pointing out items to the solicitors, who seemed in sympathy with his suspicions to see something very wrong, and to shake their heads accordingly.

For the first time, perhaps, in his life, Israel Mort did something to earn a character for politeness. He took off his hat when he had fairly got within, bowed and wished good morning all round, singling out and naming any one he knew, and reserving the most delicate bit for the last, that is to say, when addressing the chief actor in the scene.

' Mr. Griffith Williams, I am pleased to see you here so soon, and I cannot doubt but that it means bygones are to be bygones ; that we are, after all, destined it seems by fortune to pull together, and may as well therefore do it amicably.'

Was this irony, or had Israel speculated on the possibility of turning this very dangerous incident to his own advantage, by giving the offender the opportunity to back out of his ugly position, and assume a different one?

It is possible that if Griffith Williams could have given himself time for cool reflection, or if he could have got rid of the witnesses before whom he had so irretrievably committed himself, he might have responded in a spirit that, if not ' amicable,' might yet have led to a better understanding.

But his hatred of Israel was already a mania. He had no rest for it. Was it, then, to be conceived that now that he had got power, he should not use it? His reply was—

' Israel Mort, I bandy no words with you. I will pay you at a valuation the just worth of your share—'

' Which isn't in the market,' interrupted Israel, coolly.

' On your peaceably giving up possession; ' continued Mr. Williams, ignoring the interruption.

' Is that all you have to say? ' asked Israel, looking rather wistfully into the very eyes of his foe.

Griffith Williams glared at him, but disdained reply.

Taking hold of a dog-whistle that hung about his neck, a whistle familiar to every man or boy who had business in or about the mine, Israel gave full voice to it.

A sudden pattering of feet was heard a moment after, and all within the room saw outside at least a score of colliers assembled; whose threatening looks, though they were entirely unarmed, warned the gentlemen they were engaged in no child's play.

Before, however, they could obey the orders received, Israel threw up the little window and shouted—

'Stop, lads; the gentlemen, I think, are going away like gentlemen, who see they are not wanted. So let all pass, if they will, except Mr. Griffith Williams.'

Then turning round, he said to the gentlemen whom he proposed to turn out,

'I wish to speak to Mr. Griffith Williams a few words in private. I wish him distinctly to understand it is for his own sake, not mine.'

'To the devil with you!' replied Griffith; and then, turning to the others, continued, 'Come, friends, we have done enough for the day.'

'You go not, Mr. Griffith, till—'

That gentleman's reply was to bid his friends, 'Go on out!'

'Obey orders,' shouted Israel, 'All out, but *him*!'

A wild attack and scuffle, blows and vehement cries, and then Mr. Griffith's friends found themselves with torn clothes and bleeding hands and faces, not only outside, but scattered helplessly abroad, like a flock of sheep without their shepherd, while Mr. Griffith remained a prisoner in the very scene of his recent victory.

Israel had already taken possession of the cash book and hastily looked inside to see if any leaves had been torn out. Satisfied the book remained intact, he now said—

'The ledger, if you please!'

'I retain it to prove what a villain you are.'

'I tried to save your honour and respectability before, by asking you to let me speak to you alone. I still wish to save both, now you are alone. Give me the book.'

'Not while there's a drop of blood in my body to resist.'

'I warn you once more, to avoid exposure. The constable is at hand. If he comes, I charge you with burglary and theft, and I defy him to help from taking the charge.'

'You—you dare not!' gasped out Mr. Williams. 'It is a lie to frighten me; fool that you are as well as rogue!'

'Tell Crump to come in; you will find him in the engine house by the fire,' said Israel very quietly to one of his black satellites outside; and who was the man who had seen the Squire take possession of the ledger. 'Come in with him. You will be wanted as witness.' Then turning to the Squire, he said,

'Mr. Griffith Williams, once more, and for the last time will you spare yourself and me the—'

What unutterable thoughts and feelings swept through the breast of the unhappy man may be conceived, as he saw the personage approaching who had been summoned; and felt he was on the verge of he knew not what precipice, as he obeyed once more the instinct of caution that was in him, ever in him, but unfortunately never coming out of him in time, as he without a word more put down the book.'

'Thanks. And now, Mr. Williams, if you will from this moment let the subject rest, it shall never again be mentioned by me in any way. Explain to your friends as you please what has happened. I will say nothing—if not compelled to speak in defence of my character.'

The gentleman addressed picked up and put on his hat, which had fallen in the struggle, then said with lips that visibly trembled, while the frame drawn up to its fullest height seemed to assert its dignity—

'I thank you, in the *same spirit*. And since you so covet the management, take it, in return for this—this *favour* you have just done me. But I wash my hands of the matter altogether. If there are profits, I shall take my share.'

'Which I will gladly see is your full share;' interposed Israel, hardly yet understanding the exact tendency of what was said to him.

'If there are losses, those you will have to deal with as you best may, for I should allow everything to be seized before I would advance a shilling. I say this merely to meet your *friendly* advance with the like.'

' And as to the capital required ? '

' I leave all that to you.'

' You mean you will advance what is actually needed ? '

' Not a shilling. Good morning, Mr. Mort.'

He bowed ; and Israel certainly did not bow in return. All his politeness had gone out of him.

CHAPTER XXV.

REVELLING IN LAW.

ISRAEL's prospects were now dark indeed. He saw as plainly as his enemy could have explained to him the whole force of the position. He must sell his share for whatever it would fetch, if indeed any one with capital and character would buy under such circumstances; or he must move on, without aid, year after year, if that were possible, knowing that if he failed it was utter ruin; and that if he succeeded, even to the extent of being able to continue alone the costly work of reparation, there was another waiting to take the lion's share of the fruits.

But could he hope under any circumstances to make the mine so profitable as to accumulate capital for so large an undertaking?

That was the problem he revolved day by day,

now in his thoughts, now in elaborate calculations on paper, till at last he came to the conclusion it was impossible. And for this reason: he could not employ in the present dangerous state of the mine enough hands to make any noticeable difference in the amount of coal produced. Rees Thomas had already accomplished for him all that was possible in that way.

So far from his seeing any prospect of proceeding with his own bold and able scheme for the regeneration of the works, he saw, on the contrary, that to keep up even the present weekly product of coal would require unceasing expenditure on 'dead work,' so bad was the state in which it had been left by Jehoshaphat.

He had, then, simply to make up his mind to fight on for that which in the end would most likely never be obtained ; and to do so before the eyes, and in the very teeth, as it were, of a rich and influential partner, bent on his ruin, and prepared to take instant advantage of the slightest opening.

With unabated courage and fortitude he accepted the position, and sternly set himself to

confront the difficulties, whatever they might be.
His behaviour, could it have been watched by a
dispassionate and appreciative observer, would
have suggested much matter for speculation as to
what such a man might have been capable of
under happier circumstances.

The patient, sleepless care with which he followed the ever-lurking enemy—the gas—tracking
it, as a Red Indian tracks his foe, from lair to lair,
and compelling flight if he could do no more ; the
sagacity which determined how to do just that
exact amount of ' dead work ' to prevent further
' Falls ' and injuries, and at the exact time when
most needed, that would prevent calamity, and
yet not exceed by a hair's breadth the absolute
necessity of the case—all this was simply wonderful
in a man bowed down with ceaseless pecuniary
difficulty ; and who began to feel, almost for the
first time, something of an aching about the heart
whenever the subject of his domestic relations
rose to disturb the ordinary current of thought.

But he worked on so gallantly, bore all so
ungrudgingly, seemed so stable and unfaltering in
his every word and act, that even his very nume-

rous enemies began to feel a certain respect for him, though Mr. Griffith Williams was not one of the number. On the contrary, as his own personal friends cooled in their hostility to Israel, his hatred proportionately warmed to red—nay, to white-heat—fed as it was, like a fire, with fresh fuel of the most exciting kind, by seeing that as his enemy rose in public opinion, he sank.

To this cause, perhaps, may be attributed much of the litigation that very soon began again with increased fury.

First he strove for an injunction to stop Israel's proceeding with the execution of a contract he had entered into to supply the gas works with coal, his plea being that the tender had been sent in without his, Griffith Williams', authority. Had he succeeded, there would of course have been an end of Israel's management ; but when the judge had read a paper exhibited on behalf of Israel, signed by the late Mrs. Jehoshaphat, the case was stopped, and the plaintiff left with the costs.

Then he made a legal demand, with all legal formalities, for power to examine the accounts ; and it was decided that Israel had shown no unwillingness to exhibit them at a proper time; and again he had to bear all the expenses.

He tried to send a mining agent down to examine the mine, but not having asked permission, the agent was refused; and so nothing came of that move for the time being.

But when Mr. Griffith Williams went straightforwardly to work, and avowed through his lawyers his object, namely, to show that Israel was mining beyond the legitimate boundary, and actually trespassing on his, the Squire's, private estate which adjoined, Israel politely undertook not only to admit the agent, but Mr. Williams too, if he pleased to come, and offered himself to conduct them to the spot, and give every additional aid they might require to test scientifically the question. And so he came triumphant out of that, which did a little alarm him, for he was by no means sure a slight mistake of a few feet had not been made by one of his deputy officers, in securing a passage-way round an intervening and useless piece of rock.

It would be at once ludicrous and wearisome to narrate all the petty acts into which the Squire's maniacal hatred urged him to engage, in the hope of breaking down through them the resistance to his will, that could be conquered by no other means.

Israel had taken on rent a large piece of mountain land, that at one point, descending, touched the Squire's kitchen garden; and which happened at the time to be the only ground obtainable where two or three horses might be turned out on occasion. One day the garden gate was open, two of Israel's horses got in, amused themselves by eating as much as they could, and by trampling down pretty well everything else. Israel's men said the gate had been left open by the Squire's servants; the Squire brought witnesses to swear positively it had been carefully fastened at nightfall, and suggested bad feeling on the part of Israel's people as at the bottom of the affair. Israel was cast, and had to pay heavily for the damage and costs; at a time, too, when every sovereign taken from him for such purposes was like wringing out drops of his blood by a thumb-screw.

This was followed up in time by the 'right of

way' case, as it was popularly called. Israel and certain of his colliers were accustomed to pass through a field belonging to the Squire, by a path that from time immemorial had been used as a public way. Now it so happened that the Squire had done, or thought he had done, acts calculated to show it was a public path only by sufferance ; but as he had not acted on his notices, nobody stirred, or paid any attention to the matter, beyond an occasional laugh now and then, as Israel and his men were seen trudging along the path as usual.

Suddenly the Squire, having satisfied himself the path was rarely used by anybody but the colliery people, shut it up by a gate.

Next day the gate was lying on the ground, and Israel and his colliers striding over it.

Then a much more formidable affair was erected, with sharp spikes along the top ; and as if that spectacle was not sufficiently threatening, a large board with an inscription in Welsh and English appeared above the barrier, announcing that ' trespassers would be prosecuted with the utmost rigour of the law.'

About midnight of that same day that witnessed what was supposed to be the completion of the arrangement, Griffith Williams happened to look out of his bedroom window, while wondering how Israel would act on the morrow, and saw a great bonfire blazing away in a certain direction.

He dressed himself instantly, got his horse forth, and rode to the spot, where he found his anticipations verified : the heavy gate was enveloped with the flame from a great mass of brushwood, and he was just in time to see it fall in blazing ruin to the ground.

Another law-suit, and another defeat for Mr. Williams, and very heavy costs, on account of the great number of witnesses called on both sides. The right of way was established, and from that moment Israel became popular, and was regarded as a sort of tribune of the people.

How much longer this state of things would have gone on, if unchecked by some new influence, no man would have ventured to predict ; but, happily, the check came now. In severe words the judge commented on the litigating spirit shown by the facts that indirectly came out on this trial regarding the past relations of Israel and his rich partner; and though he did not directly fix on one or the other of the litigants the odium of the persecution suggested, popular opinion did, and so effectually, that the Squire was at last constrained to stop.

These proceedings of course extended through some years :—During all this time the mine was growing ever worse, till it became a byword among the colliers of other mines, when they heard of a new man going to Cwm Aber to replace some one who had gone away,

' Ah, well! if a man's hard up for a job at other places, he can always get a berth at the " Valley o' the Shadow!" meaning Israel's mine, and likening it to John Bunyan's Valley of the Shadow of Death, the ' Pilgrim's Progress ' being one of the few works of fiction a Welshman will read.

CHAPTER XXVI.

PINNED TO THE PILLOW.

IF a good man bearing himself nobly under calamity is a sight for the gods, what is it when a
man not good on the whole does the same, with
the additional burden that his moral deficiencies
impose?

Leaving casuists to answer the question, it may
be safely said that it was impossible for any one
to restrain sympathy for Israel Mort, who, knowing all the circumstances already narrated, then
heard further that Israel's wife had become gradually afflicted with some secret and inscrutable
malady, which neither Dr. Jolliffe nor any of the
more skilful practitioners of the county town
could beneficially affect; and that the only hope
of saving her was in a journey to London to see a
very eminent member of the profession who had
made his fame by dealing with kindred diseases.

Had Mrs. Mort possessed any one dear friend in the world who could have asked her in confidence the true state of the case, she would probably have burst into tears, and said simply :

' My heart is breaking, and they don't understand that ! '

But going further in confession she would, perhaps, have confided a secret to her friend that she really desired to go to London, and was glad of an excuse. The reader will guess why—to see David.

Five years have elapsed since his departure. She has heard but seldom from him. Boys away from home, in new scenes, among new acquaintances, rarely write much to those left behind. The time, too, was before postage had become cheap. Every letter cost David an amount he was often unable and sometimes unwilling to find, as depriving him of the means of relaxation from the hardships of his life.

He gave her very little knowledge of what these hardships were, very little aid of any kind by which to understand his true position, and he never once asked if his father wanted him to return, or even touched on the subject.

But his letters when they did come were still things to be wept over, to be read again and again and again, and never without some comfort. For the key-note struck by David at his departure, of hope in the future, was still sounded in these affectionate, simple, but ever earnest pages ; where the poor mother could always see in some part having reference to herself the traces of the tears that had fallen, and dimmed the words.

And it was he who, when she at last reluctantly told him of her state, which probably she would not have done, but for the vague hope that he might change his purposes and come back, or at least venture down on a visit to her—it was he who immediately drew from her sufficient knowledge concerning her ailment to be able to make inquiries as to the best adviser in London ; and so, while mentioning his name and qualifications to his mother, was led to form the wish, and urge it upon her with a passionate eloquence that no mother's heart could resist, that she would at once come up, and thus that they might meet !

The poor woman could read no farther that day.

She could only press her hand upon her heart, and go to her bed-side, and ask on her knees if indeed she might but see David her son once more, and then die.

Taking up the letter again next day, she found that David was prepared for the possibility of his father accompanying her; and if that were so, he would, if she wished, meet and take from him submissively such reception as he chose to give. She might rely on that.

But he could not conceal from her that it had been, and still was, his dearest hope to put off that meeting till he could stand in his father's presence better prepared; till, indeed, while asking forgiveness for his flight, he should be able to say without shame, 'Father, thus have I done!'

He then proceeded to show her how his father or Dr. Jolliffe might easily find some kind lady to take charge of her on the journey; and how it might be shown to the former that, through a distant acquaintance of her own in London (well known to Israel), she might be met, and taken to a lodging already provided for her, and be thoroughly well cared for during her stay; the fact being, as David took care she should well understand, he himself would attend to everything, and remain with her the whole time.

Fearing to let Israel get the least suspicion of the true originator of this idea of the journey to London, she ventured one day to ask Dr. Jolliffe if he knew such a person, mentioning the name of the physician sent to her by David.

'One of our most eminent men,' was the doctor's prompt answer. 'By-the-bye, Mrs. Mort, he is the very man I should have sent you to, had I supposed there was the least hope of your undertaking such a journey.'

'Do you think I might venture it?' said Mrs. Mort, in reply, and to the doctor's great astonishment; who knew not how his patient's usual timidity and desire to be let alone had for the moment been overborne by a stronger influence.

'Certainly I do, if only you take to it kindly yourself. All will depend on that. But how about Mr. Mort?'

'I—I think—he would not object, if he were convinced it were reasonable.'

'Indeed! Glad to hear that. If that's all, I will see him immediately.'

But Dr. Jolliffe in his own secret heart did not for a moment believe that Israel would consent. He might spare his wife, but not the money.

To his surprise he found Israel just reversed the prediction. He was more anxious about his wife than Dr. Jolliffe had thought it in his nature to be. And as to the expense, he did not even mention it.

'Unluckily,' said Israel, 'I cannot go away from the mine long enough to be with her all through.' He sighed deeply as he said this, and seemed again as if re-considering the matter. 'No, it is impossible! if anything were to happen in my absence —— No, doctor,' he said abruptly, 'that is not to be done. But if you can see your way to arrange with my wife, satisfactorily to her and to you, the money shall be forthcoming, and I shall be grateful to have it all taken off my hands.'

The doctor took him at his word, and so it was settled between them.

But after reporting his success to Mrs. Mort, and agitating her by the prospect of so soon embracing her dear boy, he seemed to forget all about the matter, or at least be very dilatory in accomplishing it. One day he spoke of the weather as unfit, and she must wait to see that settle. Another time he said he had not been fortunate enough to find any lady he knew going yet to London, but no doubt he should soon ; and so on. Poor Mrs. Mort began at last to fear she knew not what, about her husband, or her boy.

But after many days had thus passed away, he came bustling in late one night, when Israel was already in bed, to say that he had found a friend at last, who with her daughter was going to London, and that he had himself booked inside places at the coach office for the morrow ; that Israel was to leave all to him. He would fetch her in his own carriage and see her safe into the coach.

A strangely sad, yet at times happy, and altogether sleepless night followed for her. She had hardly ever travelled even in her young and vigorous days. Could she do so now with safety ?

When she left that roof, should she ever see it again? Should she in the early morning, when Israel would go as usual to the mine, take her last kiss from him, now that he seemed growing kinder to her, notwithstanding all his heavy trials?

Israel was waked by her sobbing, and then told of the journey to-morrow.

He said little, but somehow either in the few words or in the tones there was comfort; and at last under the operation of that anodyne she slept. When she woke in the morning he was gone.

But she found on the pillow a bank-note for twenty pounds, with a few words scrawled on a bit of paper, and fastened to the note by a pin.

'Dear wife,' it said, 'I don't like to disturb you; sleep will do you good. Here's twenty pounds; if you want more, let me know, and it shall reach you by next post. Come back soon, or I shall miss you; if you can also come back better in health and spirits, it shall go hard but I will try to prevent any relapse.

'Somehow, wife, adversity teaches better than prosperity, though all the same I'd be glad of a change now. God bless you,

'ISRAEL MORT.'

CHAPTER XXVII.

MOTHER AND SON.

PUNCTUAL to the very minute he had fixed, the doctor came and took off his patient towards Leath.

Mrs. Mort was too full of all she had left behind her to talk much for the first few minutes; and every effort the doctor made to rally her, to interest her, to win a smile from her, seemed only to call forth fresh fits of weeping.

So he let her grief exhaust itself, and then again tried, and with better success. She began to remark upon objects they passed, and at last ventured to ask a question about the ladies she was to accompany.

'Well,' he said, laughing, 'I have been wondering how long you would be before you asked me that. I had supposed it was not in woman's

nature to have repressed curiosity so long, about
her intended companions for so many hours, shut
up inside a coach; where, by-the-bye, you will
be all alone. You three will have it all to yourselves the whole way to London.'

'How can that be?' asked Mrs. Mort.

'Because they have taken the fourth place, to
be, as the young lady phrases it, all the more cosy.'

'Rich people, I suppose?' said Mrs. Mort, with
a sigh, and a shrinking look on her face, as if she
felt they and herself would be hardly suitable
companions.

'Yes, but very nice people, and I have no doubt
you will get on very well together. Oh, here we
are!'

They drove up to the hotel from which the
coach was to start, and upon which they were
already packing great quantities of luggage.

'Dear me,' exclaimed the doctor, 'it's later than
I thought; our friends are already in their places.
I will see your luggage safe. Come, let me intro-
duce you to them.'

Mrs. Mort went very nervously towards the
coach door, which was opened by the guard, and

there, true enough, sat two ladies, the younger of
whom, a bright-looking, lovely girl of thirteen,
seeing the astonishment depicted in Mrs. Mort's
features, clapped her hands, and said—

'Oh, that sly doctor, mamma! he has been as
good as his word, and inveigled her here under
false pretences.'

The elder lady's comment was to put out her
rosy, well-nourished hand, and grasp warmly the
attenuated fingers of the invalid, as she said—

'Dear Mrs. Mort, I am so glad! Come in.
Thank God, we have got together at last, and can
talk away to our hearts' content without the worry
of the men.'

Mrs. Mort looked from the matronly to the
maidenly face—the last more like to her a bit of
delicious sunshine than anything mortal or human,
so bright was it, so sparkling, so altogether sweet,
and her heart brimmed over as she dropped into
her seat, unable for some time to reply by a single
word.

By this time Dr. Jolliffe was back again, and
getting into the vacant place said—

'Now, Mrs. Mort, you are not going to be angry,

are you, with me, for my little surprise? It will do you good. But I must explain how it all happened. When I first knew of your proposed journey, I was aware that Mrs. Griffith Williams had long been talking of a visit to London; and so I have been manœuvring ever since to make you go together, and try together to accomplish a great and admirable work—the reconciliation of your husbands. But don't expose me, pray, to either, or you'll never have my aid again. Hark, there's the horn! Good-bye!' And with a cordial grasp all round, he disappeared, and the coach drove off.

Never surely was invalid so guarded and cared for as was Mrs. Mort now by her two friends. Nest sat opposite her, and seemed to do nothing but study her face, as if to discover what it was likely to want or think next. As to Mrs. Griffith Williams, she made the invalid lean against her, took her poor thin cold fingers into her own, and warmed them tenderly, and continued to retain them afterwards.

Is it to be wondered at, then, if before an hour or two had passed away, all the hidden troubles in the hearts of the two women had been brought forth, in sympathetic exchange, and each left the better for the process?

Or that even the one little secret which at first the poor mother thought it best, even for David's sake, to conceal, that she was going to meet him, came out at last; and was welcomed by Mrs. Griffith Williams with significant gladness, and by Nest's falling into a brown study, which never quite left her all the way to London.

Would they know him? How would he be dressed? Was he tall, thin, or stout? Would he know them?

Mrs. Mort said simply she was sure she and he would know each other, and she thought he would know Mrs. Griffith, but was quite sure he would never recognize in the richly dressed young lady opposite (who was indeed in appearance already verging on womanhood in spite of her tender years), the little girl who had played with him in the wood of Brynnant.

Nest did not seem to like this idea, and was very sure she would know him.

The pleasurable excitement of these revelations,

and of the interchange of friendly feeling, was followed by the usual reaction ; and it became necessary to stop for the night.

Mrs. Mort would have had them go on without her, but was made to feel herself so ashamed of the proposition, as to venture no more proposals of the kind.

In the morning she was better. And the remainder of the journey was pursued almost in silence, each one getting occupied with her own thoughts.

They were already passing through the crowded streets of London, and had nearly reached the inn where the coach stopped, when Nest suddenly exclaimed—

'There he is! Look! Do look, Mrs. Mort. In the blue coat! See how anxiously he is watching the coach in advance of us. It must be he!'

Mrs. Mort tried to look, but there was a watery film over her eyes that blinded them. She was willing to believe it was he, and could wait patiently, blessing God the while that the time had come she had so long prayed for.

The inn yard was reached, and there at the

very corner, and on the edge of the kerb stone, stood a manly-looking youth of seventeen or eighteen, with a nervous sensitive face, and wonderfully bright eyes, that were fixed anxiously on the window of the coach, as it passed round the corner.

' Mother ! ' rang out a clear voice, and a hand was lain on the edge of the window, while its owner ran along by the side, though there was scarcely room for him to do so without danger.

' Take care, Oh my dear boy ! ' responded Mrs. Mort, rising for a moment to touch his hand, but obliged to fall back for weakness.

' All right, mother, don't fear ! '

The moment the coach stopped he opened the door, and taking no notice of any one but his mother, he lifted her slight figure in his arms, and carried her away without a word to a hackney coach in waiting, and deposited her inside ; and was then locked in her arms, and so long, that it seemed she knew not how again to let him go. But at last she remembered her friends.

' Oh, Mrs. Williams, and Nest ! ' she said, as if grieved at her own forgetfulness.

'You don't mean, mother——'

'Yes, dear, and they have taken such care of
me. Go to them; I can wait now; go, David, but
don't be long. Stop!' He did stop, feeling how
deep, how passionate was the cry that came out
of his mother's soul in that one word. So there
was another prolonged embrace, and then he was
allowed to go.

How he excused himself to the ladies he never
told his mother, but when he came back his face
was crimsoned, and his eyes glowing with excitement, as he explained how kindly he had been
received, and how astonished he was at the change
in Nest; that, indeed, he had not been able to
recognise her till she laughed, and said one of her
old saucy things to him.

He had given them his mother's address, and
they were to call each day to see her, and they
insisted on taking her back with them to Wales.

Happy hours, happy days, were those that
succeeded, for both mother and son; for though
she had to tell him of his father's troubles, and of
the ever increasing danger of some calamity in
connection with the mine, and although he had

to tell her of the bitternesses of life to a friendless boy set down in the vast wilderness of London—these were matters already anticipated and known something about; whereas, the fact of their being again together, the overflowing love that seemed to each a new life, a kind of heaven on earth suddenly revealed to two hearts that were in the sorest need of such consolation—these were the influences predominant now, and that for the time overmastered all else.

The physician was seen, and the case very thoughtfully gone into. And the decision given after a second visit was, that she had better return home as soon as her friends were ready, and that she should take with her suggestions for the use of Dr. Jolliffe, that he thought might fairly be expected to do her good and protract her life, probably for some years, though cure itself was not to be expected.

And with such cold comfort as this gave, mother and son were obliged to be content.

The two families met daily, and Nest and David were thus once again thrown into each other's society. But it was curious that while David,

who at first in the frank innocence of his heart
could not help letting it be seen that he had
practically forgotten Nest altogether, began now
only too keenly to remember her, and to find
himself miserable whenever Nest was away; Nest,
on the contrary, who had shown her delight in
being the first to see and to point him out,
gradually relapsed into silence, or worse, to mono-
syllables.

Then he felt he could speak no more. All the
realities of his position, as a clerk at eighteen
shillings a week, pressed in upon him with overwhelming force, and made him at last ready to
welcome the hour of the departure.

And when that time came and his mother wept
on his neck, she whispered to him, 'David, darling,
when I am gone, there is, I hope, another mother
for you. I must not say more; all the rest is with
you and with God. Bless you, my boy; keep good
and true, and do not fear work, and if—if—we
do never meet again in this world——'

'Oh, we shall, mother; we shall!' said David,
kissing away the tears that were rolling down the
pale wasted cheeks. 'For my sake it must be so.

Wait, dearest mother, wait to see what I will make of myself; how I will come back to you in yet another half-dozen years, a man, and with a man's record of genuine work done! Oh, mother, are you not the very dearest thing on earth to me? Then God bless you, and keep you safe for that day!'

And so they parted. David shook hands with Mrs. Griffith Williams, but was so nervous about what else remained to do, that he started like a guilty thing when that lady said with a smile—

'Come, David, shake hands with Nest, who has been crying her eyes out all night.'

'Oh, mother!' exclaimed Nest's deprecatory voice, while she looked even more guilty than David.

The hands were, however, locked in each other just for one single moment; but that moment was long enough for David and Nest to see in each other's eyes a something that for days, months, years afterwards, would not be forgotten by either.

CHAPTER XXVIII.

THE LAST CALL.

The return journey was managed without breaking it for a night's rest; and warm were the
congratulations that welcomed Mrs. Mort when
met by the doctor; who, as well as Israel, had
received notice of the time of her coming. After
a most touching and grateful good bye to her
friends, he took her home.

As he set her down in her own house once more,
and left her after a little genial chat, and the expression of a still more decided hope of recovery
than the London physician had given, she gazed
around her as if all that had intervened since she
last sat there was a dream.

'When would Mr. Mort be home?' she asked
the servant; who could tell her nothing, but that
she expected he would be late, as he was so very
busy.

She had tea prepared, but found all appetite had passed away.

She must go upstairs to her bed-room. She went there with the girl's aid, and began to open drawers, and sort things, and arrange them in her own fashion where she found any change.

There seemed a kind of mania upon her for looking after things she had not seen for many years, and for pausing over them, sometimes putting them to her lips before she put them down.

Thus she came upon certain relics of childhood, not David's only, but of the two little ones resting in the churchyard by the wild stream. And she examined them with a strange feeling that somehow they looked altered, and that she was worried about their identity.

Then suddenly sitting down, she began to wring her hands, and cry aloud—

' Israel, my husband, come ! '

The cry was answered from below—

' Mary ! '

She heard the heavy step, she rose to meet it, she advanced, but tottered, and was falling, when

Israel's arm caught and encircled her, and feeling her grow more and more heavy, carried her to the bed, and lifted her on to it, and then kissed her.

'What, wife, overcome by the journey! Don't mind! That'll soon pass away. Come, tell me all about it; but I see you are not strong enough to-night. To-morrow then. I am in no mood to eat, so I shall come to bed.'

The faintest possible sound came to his ear of—
'Israel!'

He had moved away, but warned by that sound he turned, and strode to the bed-side, and took one hand in his, while the other slid under her back, and enfolded her waist.

'Israel!' then for some seconds she could say no more, for the under-current of restrained anguish at what she was going to say. 'I—I have seen David—forgive him—and me—for—I —am dying—dear—dear husband.'

'No, no, no! a thousand times no! I do forgive him and you. Wife, wife! this is an ill time for me. I can no longer spare you; believe me, I cannot. See, drink this, the cordial!'

With shut eyes, she blindly pushed away the proffered glass, then murmured—

'Oh, I have so much to say, and—and—Israel— light the candle, it is so dark! Where are you?' The moment she felt his hand, she kissed it passionately, lifted her face heavenward, and seemed silently to struggle with herself.

'Oh God, bless him, and make smooth his path! Oh, dear God, oh, Christ, bless my husband and my——'

Israel heard no more; he covered his eyes, as if ashamed of that which they were revealing. When he uncovered them it was to see his wife's dead features, smiling on him in death.

END OF THE SECOND VOLUME.

LONDON: PRINTED BY
SPOTTISWOODE AND CO., NEW-STREET SQUARE
AND PARLIAMENT STREET

www.ingramcontent.com/pod-product-compliance
Lightning Source LLC
Chambersburg PA
CBHW031343070726
47496CB00017B/1637